The IMMATURE Lover and Other Stories

Lost Stories Rewritten

Henry Turner

Email: okeyjedi@gmail.com

Cover design *by* Rawpixel.com - Freepik.com

Model 1: Benzoix - Freepik.com

Model 2: by Sound on – pexels.com.com

Cover modification by Aziujali Okechukwu

ISBN 978-978-791-544-8

Dedication

I dedicate this work to Yahweh Sabaoth, who every magnificent gift and every perfect gift comes from. Your loving kindness has for ever been present in my life.

Acknowledgments

First and foremost, I would like to say thank you to Yahweh Sabaoth for his ever loving kindness to me; everything I achieve is a result of what you do' I am noting without you.

I would also like to thank the great minds who have laid the ground works many years ago, which I am now exploiting, great minds like Guy de Maupassant, Erckmann-Chatrian, Kate Chopin, Otto Larssen, Leo Tolstoy, John Strange Winter, Bernhard Severin, Lucy Maud Montgomery, Ferencz Molnar, and Fiodor M. Dostoyevsky. Reading and rewriting their works gave me more knowledge and inspiration than I could ever get in any school. You guys are no longer with us, but your works are seeds that are continually planted in the minds of generations upon generation. Your works have immortalized you in us and in many others who have learned from you without meeting you in person. Thank you.

Contents

The Immature Lover

Sophie was waiting under the apple tree at the gate for Stephen Keaton. She was engaged to him, and he always come to see her on Saturday and Wednesday evenings. The sun has set, and the air was mellow and warm. Against the lemon-tinted sky, the trees along the walk and the tall Birches in the background stood out darkly. The breath of mint floated out from the compound, and a light rain like dew was falling.

Sophie leaned against the gate, listening for the sound of a car and dreamily watching the light shining out from the window of Vivian Elora's room. The window blind was up and she could see Miss Elora writing at her table. Her image was distinct against the light. Elora is a movie actress and has appeared in about a dozen of it.

Sophie reflected without the least envy that Miss Elora was very beautiful. She had never seen anyone who was really as beautiful as her before. Her beauty is indescribable, like that of a goddess, just as she appears in her movies. Sophie has watched all of Elora's movies. Sophie Trevor believe she is not pretty herself. But in reality she is a nice-looking girl, with clear eyes, rosy cheeks, and a pervading air of content and happiness her life had always known. She is an orphan and raised by (her mother's sister) her aunt and her husband. In summer, they sometimes go on a vacation for a week or two, but this year Miss Elora has visited them. She had been with them about a week. She is a Hollywood actress and has with her all the glamour, but her entire life is an enigma. Nothing was known about her. The Trevors liked her well enough as a guest. Sophie admired and held her in awe. She wondered what Stephen would think of this beautiful lady, if they meet when he arrive.

It was quite dark when he came. Sophie opened the gate for him, and he got out of his car and walked up the lane beside her with his arm about her. Miss Elora had moved to the living room where she was singing, accompanying herself on the piano. Sophie felt annoyed. The living room was considered her private domain on Wednesday and Saturday night, but Miss Elora did not know that.

“Who is singing?” asked Stephen. “What a voice she has!”

“That’s our new guest, Miss Elora,” answered Sophie. “She’s an actress and sings and does everything. She is so beautiful, Stephen.”

“Yah?” said the young man indifferently.

He was not in the least interested in the Trevor’s new guest. Indeed, he considered her presence a nuisance. He pressed Sophie closer to him, and when they reached the gate, he kissed her. Sophie always remembered that moment afterwards. She was so supremely happy.

Stephen went off to park his car well, and Sophie waited for him on the porch steps, wondering if any other girl in the world could be as happy as she is, or love anyone as much as she loved Stephen. She did not see how it could be possible, because there was only one Stephen.

When Stephen came back, she took him into the living room, half shyly, half proudly. He was a handsome fellow with a magnificent physique. Miss Elora stopped singing and turned around on the piano stool as they entered. The room is shining with a mellow light from the pink electric lamp on the table. The light reflected on her beautiful dress. She wore a dress of crepe, cut low in the neck and open at the back. Sophie had never seen anyone dressed so before. To her, it seemed immodest.

She introduced Stephen. He bowed awkwardly to her as if she was an European royal and sat stiffly down by the window with his eyes riveted on Miss Elora's face. Sophie, catching a glimpse of herself in the old-fashioned mirror above the mantel, suddenly felt an icy chill of dissatisfaction. Her figure had never seemed to her so stout and stiff, her brown hair so dull and prim, her complexion so muddy, her features so lanky. She wished Miss Elora would go out of the room.

Vivian Elora watched the two faces before her; a hard gleam, half mockery, half malice, flashed into her eyes and a smile crept about her lips. She looked straight into Stephen Keaton's naïve brown eyes and read the young man's dazzled admiration. There was contempt in the look she turned on by Sophie.

"You were singing when we came in," said Stephen. "Won't you go on, please? I am very fond of music."

Miss Elora turned again to the piano. The gleaming curves of her neck and shoulders rose out of their filmy sheathing of lace. Stephen, sitting where he could see her face with its rose-leaf colored make-up and golden hair clustering about it, gazed at her. Sophie saw how he was looking at her. She suddenly began to hate the black-eyed witch at the piano to fear her as well. Why did Stephen look at her like that? She wished she had not brought him in at all. She felt small and angry, and wanted to cry.

Vivian Elora went on singing, drifting from one sweet love song into another. Once she looked up at Stephen Keaton. He rose quickly and went to her side, looking down at her with a strange fire in his eyes.

Sophie was shocked by the way Stephen acted; she got up abruptly and left the room. She was angry, bitter, and jealous, but she thought Stephen would follow her. When he did not, she could not believe it. She waited on the porch for him, not knowing whether she was more angry or miserable. She would not go back into the room. Vivian Elora had stopped singing. She could hear an inaudible murmur of voices. When she had waited there an hour, she went upstairs to her room with ostentatious footsteps. She was too angry to cry or to realize what had happened and still kept hoping for all sorts of impossible things as she sat by her window.

It was ten o'clock when Stephen went away and Vivian Elora passed up the hall to her room. Sophie clenched her hands in an orgy of helpless rage. She was very angry, but under her fury was a horrible ache of pain. It was just about three hours ago she had been so happy! It must be more than that! What had happened? Had she made a fool of herself? Maybe I didn't behave the way I should. Perhaps Stephen had come out to look for her after she had gone upstairs and, not finding her, had gone back to Miss Elora to show her he was angry. This poor hope was a minor comfort. She wished she had not acted as she had. It looked spiteful and jealous, and Stephen did not like people who were spiteful and jealous. She would show him she was sorry if he came back, and everything would be all right.

She laid awake most of the night, thinking out plausible reasons and excuses for Stephen's behavior, and trying to convince herself that she had exaggerated everything absurdly. Towards morning she fell asleep and awoke, hardly remembering what had happened. Then it rolled back upon her crushingly.

But she rose and dressed in better spirits. It had been hardest to lie there and do nothing. Now the day was before her and something pleasant might happen. Stephen might come back in the evening. She would be doubly nice to him to make up.

Mrs. Trevor looked sharply at her niece's dull eyes and pale cheeks at the breakfast table. She had her own thoughts about things. She is a fat, beautiful woman with a rather harsh face.

"Did you go upstairs last night and leave Stephen Keaton with Miss Elora?" she asked bluntly.

"Yes," muttered Sophie.

"Did you have a quarrel with him?"

"No."

"What made you act so queer?"

"I couldn't help it," faltered the girl.

The food she was eating seemed to choke her. She wished she were a hundred miles away from everyone she ever knew.

Mrs. Trevor gave a grunt of dissatisfaction.

"Well, I think it is a pretty queer piece of business. But if you are satisfied, it isn't anyone else's concern, I suppose. He stayed with her till ten o'clock and when he left, she did everything but kiss him. She asked him to come back, too. I heard."

"Aunt!" protested the girl.

She felt as if her aunt were striking her blow after blow on a sensitive spot. It was bad enough to know it all, but to hear it put into such cold, brutal words was more than she could endure. It seemed to make everything so horribly sure.

"I guess I had a right to listen, don't I, she asked, with such going on in my own house? You're a little fool, Sophie! You gave Vivian the leeway to take advantage of your childish mentality. I wish I'd never taken her in, and if you say so, I'll send her packing right away and not give her a chance to make mischief at you people."

Sophie's suffering found vent in a burst of anger, but she managed to reply;

"You needn't do anything of the sort!" she cried.

"It's all nonsense about Stephen. It's not my fault anyhow, if he is so easily led away as that, I am sure I don't want him! I wish, Aunt, you'd leave me alone!"

"Oh, very well!" replied Mrs. Trevor in an offended tone. "It was for your own good I spoke. You know best, I suppose. If you don't care, I don't know that anyone else should."

Sophie went about her work looking so dejected. A great hatred had sprung up in her heart against Vivian. The simple-hearted girl felt almost murderous. The whole day seemed like a nightmare to her. In the evening, Sophie dressed herself, most delicately, hoping that Steve will surely visit her again, but he did not; she retired to bed that night, feeling so much troubled. It seems as if she will not live through the night. She lay staring wide-eyed through the darkness until dawn. She wished that she might cry, but no tears came to her relief. She kept looking at her cell phone, hoping maybe he would call or at list chart her up, but he didn't. She just can't think of a friend to chart with because all she always had is Stephen. Being introversive in nature, she hardly charts with her other friends.

Next day she went to her house chore with furious energy. When her usual tasks were done, she ransacked the house for other work to engage herself. She was afraid if she stopped work for a moment, she would go mad. Mrs. Trevor watched her with so much pity.

That evening she walked to prayer meeting in the schoolhouse about half a mile away. She never misses attending those meeting, and Stephen was mostly on hand to see her home. He was not there tonight. She wished she had not come. It was dreadful to have to sit still and think. She did not hear a word the minister said.

She had to walk home with a crowd of girls; she pretended to be happy and jovial so that none of the girls might suspect her troubles. She was also tortured by the fear that everyone knew her shame and humiliation and pitied her. She noticed that one of the girls, Aviana, kept looking at her. Underneath all she was trying to assign a satisfactory reason for Stephen not showing up. He had not always kept to his promise, and of course he was a little cross at her, as was natural. If he had come before, she could have gone down in the very dust at his feet and implored for his forgiveness.

When she reached home, she went into the compound and sat down. The coolness of the night soothed her. She felt happier and more hopeful. The recollection comforted her because she thought over all that had passed between her and Stephen. She was at peace when she went in.

Tomorrow is Sunday; she thought when she woke up in the morning. Her step was lighter and her face brighter. Mrs. Trevor seemed to be in a bad mode. She said bluntly,

“Do you know that Stephen Keaton was here last night?”

Sophie felt the cold tighten round her heart. Yet underneath it sprang up a wild, sweet hope.

"Stephen here! I suppose he forgot it was a prayer-meeting night. What did he say? Why didn't you tell him where I was?"

"I don't think he forgot it was prayer meeting night," returned Mrs. Trevor with measured emphasis. "'It didn't look like his memory failed him after-all, because he did not ask of your whereabout. He took good care to go before you got home, too. Miss Elora entertained him. I guess she was quite capable of it."

Sophie bent over her dishes in silence. Her face was deadly white.

"I'll send her away," said Mrs. Trevor pityingly. "When she's gone, Stephen will soon come back to you."

"No, you won't!" said Sophie fiercely. "If you do, she will only go over and lodge at Barstows Hotel, and it would be worse than ever. I don't care at all about them both, I don't care! As for Stephen coming back to me, do you think I want him anymore? He's welcome to go."

"He's only just fooled by her pretty face," persisted Mrs. Trevor in a clumsy effort at comforting her. "She's just turning his head, and he isn't really in his right senses. You'll see, he'll be ashamed of himself when he comes to them again. He knows very well in his heart that you're worth ten girls like her."

Sophie turned around to face her aunt.

"Aunt," she said desperately, "you mean well, I know, but you're killing me! I can't stand it. For God's sake, don't say another word to me about this, no matter what happens. And don't keep looking at me as if I were a victim! She watches us and it would please her to think I cared. I don't, and I mean to make I don't. I guess I'm well rid of a fellow as fickle as he is, and I've sense enough to know it."

As she was climbing upstairs, her cell phone started to beep. Somebody just charted her on the social media. It was Aviana, and her message just stated 'do you know?' then pictures of Vivian and Stephen having a romantic moment in a bar started appearing on her social media page one after another. She couldn't respond to the post. She was consumed with a mixed feeling of rage and sorrow. As she climbed the steps, she ripped off her engagement ring from her fingers. All sorts of wild ideas flashed through her head. She would go down and confront Vivian Elora or would rush off and find Stephen and throw his ring at him, no matter where he was, or maybe she would go away where no one would ever see her again. Why can't she just die? Was it likely people could suffer like this and yet go on living?

"I don't care—don't care!" she moaned, telling the lie aloud to herself, as if she hoped that by this means she would come to believe it.

When it was twilight, she went out to the front steps and leaned her aching head against the tree in the compound resting under its shadows. The sun had just set and the whole world swam in dusky golden light. The wonderful beauty of nature frightened her. She felt like a blot on it.

While she stood there, a car came driving up the lane and wheeled about on the steps. In it was Stephen Keaton. This wasn't his car but his father's car, obviously trying to show off the more in other to impress Elora.

Sophie saw him and, in spite of the maddening throb of hope that surged suddenly to transfigure the world for her, her pride rose in arms. Had Stephen come the night before, he would have found her loving and humble. Even now, had she but been sure that he had come to see her, she would have forgiven him. But was it the other? The torturing doubt stung her like a scorpion.

She waited, stubbornly resolved that she would not speak first. It was not in her place. Stephen stopped his car sharply. He dared not look at Sophie, but he felt her uncompromising attitude. He was miserably ashamed of himself, and he felt angry at Sophie for his shame.

"Do you care to come for a drive?" he asked awkwardly, with a covert glance at the living room windows.

Sophie caught the glance, and her jealous perception instantly divined its true significance. Her heart died within her. She did not care what he said.

"Oh," she cried with a toss of her head, "it's not me you want, Miss Elora, isn't it? She's away at the mall. You'll find her there, if I must say."

Still, in spite of all, she perversely hoped. If he would only make any sign, the least in the world, that he is sorry, that he still loved her, she would forgive him for everything. When he drove away without another word, she could not believe it. Surely he would not go; he knew she did not mean it. Maybe he would turn back before he got to the gate.

But he did not. Around the turn of the road, she saw him disappear. She could not see if he took the mall lane further on, but she was sure he would. She was furious at herself for acting as she had done. It was all her fault again! Oh, if he would only give her another chance!

Later, she was in her room when she heard the car drive up again. She knew it was Stephen and that he had brought Vivian Elora home. Acting on a sudden wild impulse, the girl stepped out on the landing and confronted her rival as she came up the stairs.

The latter paused at the sight of the white face and anguished eyes. There was a little mocking smile on her lovely face.

"Elora," said Sophie in a quivering voice, "what do you mean by all this? You know I'm engaged to Stephen Keaton!"

Miss Elora laughed softly.

"Really? If you are engaged to the young man, my dear Sophie, I would advise you to look after him more sharply. He seems very willing to flirt, I should say."

She passed on to her room with a malicious smile. Sophie shrank back against the wall, humiliated and baffled. When she found herself alone, she crawled back to her room and threw herself face downward on the bed, praying that she might die.

But she had to live through the horrible month that followed, a month so full of agony that she seemed to draw every breath in pain. It seemed Miss Elora have decided to live permanently with them and as for Stephen, he never sought her again; he went everywhere with Miss Elora. His infatuation was the talk of the town. Sophie knew that her story was in everyone's mouth, and her pride destroyed; but she carried a brave look outwardly. No one could believe she cared. Thanks to social media, she made new friends who live in many countries who knew neither her nor her predicament. She drowns her pain with endless chats. Seeing the two together no longer strikes her like a lightning bolt, but it feels more like a chronic pain that must be endured.

She believed that the actress was merely deluding Stephen for her own amusement and would never dream of marrying him. But one day the idea occurred to her that she might. Sophie had always told herself that even if Stephen wanted to come back to her, she would never take him back, but now, by the horror that came over her, she knew how strong her mistake had really been and despised herself more than ever.

One evening, she was alone in the living room. She had just switched on the big bright light (which is hardly switched on) and was listlessly arranging the room. She looked old and worn out. Her color was gone and her eyes were dull. As she worked, the door opened and Vivian Elora walked in or, rather, reeled into the room.

Sophie dropped the book she held and gazed at her as one in a dream. The actress's face was flushed and her hair was wildly disordered. Her eyes glittered with an unearthly light. She was talking incoherently. The air was heavy with the fumes of hot drink.

Sophie laughed hysterically at the sight. Vivian Elora was grossly intoxicated. This woman whom Stephen Keaton worshiped, for whom he had forsaken her, was reeling about the room, laughing idiotically, talking wildly in a thick voice and dancing erotically. If he could but see her now!

Sophie turned white with the passion of the wild idea that had come to her. Stephen Keaton should see this woman in her true colors. She lost no time. Swiftly she left the room and locked the door behind Vivian, the maudlin babbling creature still inside. Then she flung a shawl over her head and ran from the house. It was not far from the Keaton homestead. She ran all the way, hardly knowing what she was doing. But along the way, as she was panting, she stopped to think, and another idea came into her head, so she ran back to her house. She got her cell phone and went back to the living room and started recording Vivian as she keeps reeling herself around, talking incoherently and even trying to dance erotically, pulling her clothes up now and then to flash her biological private belongings. Sophie mounted her phone on a position which it can record Vivian where ever she is in the living room, then she went to the floor where Vivian had dropped her pause, picked it up and pulled out her cell phone. She hurriedly searched for Stephen's cell phone number, which she knew of head, and then, with Vivian's number, she sent a message to Stephen:

'My love, hurry up to the Keaton residence where I am, please. You are to come at once. It is an emergency!'

Ten minutes have not yet passed when Stephen arrived, on see him Sophie hurriedly unlocks the living. She opened the door immediately before he knocked. He busted in, looking rather confusingly at Sophie, who is looking at him with a mocking smile.

Seeing Sophie's mocking smile, he was full of fear. Had Sophie gone out of her mind? Had she done anything to Elora? Had she?–

"Where is Elora? Has anything happened to her?" cried Stephen savagely. "Is she ill? What is the matter?" He asked.

"She's in the living room," she said wildly. "Go in and see her, Stephen."

As he entered, the actress on seeing him reeled to her feet and restarted her erotic dance towards him. He stood and gazed at her stupidly. This could not be Vivian, this creature reeking with alcohol, dancing unconventional, uttering such foolish words! What fiend was this in her likeness?

He grew sick at heart and brain; she had her arms about him. He tried to push her away, but she clung closer, and her senseless laughter echoed through the room.

She said to him, "My latest catch, I hope your thing is as big as you look? Are you sure you can satisfy a big girl like me? Hum! I once took 3 guys down at once, you know, come on stop being a baby, what's that look on your face for? Hum! Scared of mummy? Haha haha! Okay! okay! I understand, I all explain. Haha haha! I was with 2 guys and we only had a threesome, but they were not good enough. Okay, now! Show me what you got, let me see how good you are".

He grew sicker at heart and brain. Before he could say a word, she started to cough and before he knew what to make of this; she vomited on his face and body. He flung her from him with an effort and rushed out through the hall and down the road like a madman with her vomit dripping down all over him. And all along, Sophie was recording everything with her phone in the corner. She felt that she had properly avenged herself. She was glad with a joy more pitiful than grief.

The next day Vivian Elora was so ashamed of what happened that she left the house before 9am. Mrs. Trevor suspecting some mystery behind her sudden departure, so she questioned Sophie sharply, but could find out nothing. The girl kept her own secret stubbornly.

Sophie now goes anywhere she wants with an air of a soldier who is feared by her enemies for having a detonator in her pocket. As a means to entertain herself, she edited clips of her recordings and, like a daily memo, sent it to Elora one each day. Elora being terrified how this could damage her image. Sent a lot of apologetic messages to Sophie, but she won't respond. She called her on the phone over a thousand times, but she won't budge. Then, within a few days, she sent her an expensive necklace. But Sophie refused to accept it. Elora kept on sending her message, even promising to make her a star in Hollywood if she would only give up her vengeful prank and delete these destructive recordings.

On the other hand, Mrs. Trevor noticed that her nice seemed to be happier these days. She sings and dances while working; she devours her meals and even strikes up conversation with her, something she had quit since the turn of events. She now dresses fancifully like an actress, and doesn't miss any gathering or events. Mrs. Trevor tried to pressure her to spill the beans, but she won't.

Stephen Keaton was so ashamed he hardly comes out of the house. On one occasion, he came to church where he was sure to see Sophie because she never misses any. He sat in the pew with his eyes fixed on her; it was quite clear to everyone, even the minister, that he heard not a word of the sermon because his head was permanently fixed on Sophie. He was so emaciated and horrible looking: his eyes hallow and dark, his face pale white, he had the appearance of a zombie that has not fed for two weeks after his resurrection. The whole church was concerned about his health. After the church service, when everybody was exchanging pleasantries outside, he approached Sophie, wanting to talk to her, but she snobbishly brushed him of saying, “Hi Stephen! How are you doing” touching his chicks she walked on. Everybody was in complete observation of this, even the minister, and it was as if everybody's eyes were pleading to her on his behalf for forgiveness.

On getting home, Sophie was surprised that the Minister and Stephen’s mother were already at her home talking with her aunty in the living room. They invited her to join them, but she refused. The Minister stood up and said, “My dear child, it is clear that you are very much aware of the reason why we are here.” Sophie made no comment, but just kept her calm.

The Minister continued, “I can see there is no need trying to talk to you now, since you are not in the mode for it but do consider when ever your anger drops down that ‘to err is human but to forgive is divine.’ Never let vengeance turn you into the very monster you are trying to avenge.”

On saying so, he got up to leave but Stephen’s mother wanted them to sit and persuade the young girl but he said, “No, let her be, she too has suffered but endured it courageously.”

After they left, Mrs. Trevor was about to question her nice seriously when on the door stood Vivian Elora looking ghostly. Sophie, knowing what she came for, got up and, with a mocking smile, excused herself to change her church attire. She got up and walked to her room with a dancing step, as if some unseen ghosts were playing sweet tones for her.

After some couple of minute when she came down the steps, the look on her aunt's face was clear that Elora has downloaded everything on her. Her aunty was the one to speak first. "Sophie darling please come"

Sophie responded, "I know—I know the party is over." She handed her phone over to her aunty and said: "Do it yourself. It's a folder inside the video folder titled 'Vivian's hit movie'." Her aunty took the phone from her, opened the folders as she was told, and gave it to Elora. She stared at the contents with terror in her eyes and deleted everything with a great sigh of relief. Then both of them turned to Sophie and looked at her with something in their minds but she understood and said: "Don't worry about it, I didn't find it necessary to make copies of it and by the living God I haven't posted it anywhere except your social media page."

At this Vivian Elora stood up and said: "I owe you a lot for this. Pardon me for what I did. It is a normal where I work. If you need anything, please don't hesitate to call." She thanked Mrs. Trevor and took her leave.

Mrs. Trevor looked at Sophie with an air of delight and said, "You strong headed, stubborn girl, that was brave but risky. Please don't do that again. She got up huge her and said, "Do finish what you started."

The interest and curiosity of the neighborhood centered around Stephen Keaton, and his story was well discussed. Gossip said that the actress had jilted him and that he was so ashamed and heartbroken about it. Then came the rumor that he was going to hide permanently in New York.

Sophie heard it apathetically. Life seemed ended for her. There was nothing to look forward to. She could not even look back. All the past was embittered. The last day she meet Stephen was that day at the church service. She sometimes wondered what he must think of her for what she had done. Did he think she was a wicked and heartless person? She did not care. It was rather a relief to hear that he was going away. She would not be tortured by the fear of meeting him again. She was sure he would never come back to her. If he did, she would never forgive him.

One evening in early September, Sophie was loitering along the street towards the evening. She had worked slavishly all day and was very tired, but she was loath to go into the house, where her trouble always seemed to weigh on her more heavily. The dusk, sweet night seemed to soothe her as it always did.

She leaned her head against the tree by the gate. How long Stephen Keaton had been standing by her she did not know, but when she looked up, he was there. In the dim light, she could see how haggard and hollow-eyed he had grown. He had changed almost as much as herself. He looked like a terribly sick patient just discharged from the hospital.

The girl's first proud impulse was to turn coldly away and leave him. But some strange tumult in her heart kept her still. What had he come to say?

There was a moment's silence. Then Stephen spoke in a muffled voice.

"I couldn't go away without seeing you once more, Sophie, to say goodbye. Perhaps you won't speak to me. You must hate me. I deserve it."

He paused, but she said no word. She could not. After a space, he went wistfully on.

"I know you can never forgive me. I've behaved like a fool. There isn't any excuse I can give for my stupidity. I don't think I could have been in my right senses, Sophie. It all seems like some bad dream now. When I saw her that night, I came to my right mind, and I've been the most miserable man alive ever since. Not for her, but because I'd lost you. I can't bear to live here any longer, so I am going away. Will you say goodbye, Sophie?"

Still, she did not speak. There are so many things she wanted to say, but she could not say them. Did he mean that he loved her still? If she were sure of that, she could forgive him for anything, but her doubt rendered her mute.

The young man turned away despairingly from her rigid attitude. So be it. He had brought his fate to himself.

He had gone but a few steps when Sophie suddenly found her voice with a gasp.

“Stephen!” He came swiftly back. “Oh, Stephen, do you still love me?”

He caught her hands in his.

“Love you, Sophie, yes, yes! I always have. That other wasn’t love, it was just madness. When it passed, I hated life because I’d lost you. I know you can’t forgive me, but, oh–”

He broke down and began to cry. Sophie flung her arms around his neck and put her face up to his. She felt as if her heart must break with its great happiness. He understood her mute pardon. In their kiss, the past was put aside. Sophie’s months of grief and agony have ended.

The End.

The Amateur Lover

There is a young man by the name of Cassidy Porter. He is a civil servant in the department of education and live Boston, Massachusetts. He usually uses the public transport to his place of work every morning and every day he always sits opposite a particular girl, with whom he later fell in love with.

She is a salesgirl in a shopping center and usually goes to work at the same time every day. She is fair in complexion, with a somewhat sparkling dark eyes. He always sees her coming at the corner of the same street, and every day she always run in other to catch-up with the bus because she is always late to work, and in other not to miss the bus she have to jump on the steps like an athlete before the wheels had quite stopped. Then she goes inside, out of breath, sits down and observes the people round.

The first time that he saw her, Cassidy loved her face and figure. She was the kind of girl he long to be with. She was the girl of his fantasy. She seemed to respond to some chord in his being, to that sort of ideal love which one longs for in the depths of the heart, but is too ashamed to let it out.

He looked at her intently, not meaning to be rude, and she became embarrassed and blushed. He noticed it, tried to turn away his eyes; but he involuntarily fixed them upon her again, over and over, even when he tried to look in another direction. In a few days, they seemed to know each other without having spoken. He gave up his sit to her when the bus was full and stood up against his own comfort. In a short time, she had become so familiar with him as to greet him with a little smile; although she always dropped her eyes under his constant gaze, which she felt were too ardent, yet she did not feel offended at being looked at in such a manner.

One day, they opened up by speaking to each other. A rapid friendship became established between them, and it became a daily routine of half an hour. That was certainly the sweetest half hour in Cassidy's life. He thought of her all the rest of the day, saw her image continually during the long office hours. It was as if he was charmed by that strong and ever presence recollections, those impressions of love stamped on his heart by that lovely stranger, and it seemed to him that if he could win this girl's love it would be his highest achievement, his love for her is beyond expression .

Every morning she now shake hands with him, and he preserved the scent of that touch and the memory of the gentle pressure of her little fingers until the next day, and he almost fancied that he preserved the imprint on his palm. He anxiously waited for this big bus ride every day, while Sundays seemed too lonely and heartbreaking days. However, there was no doubt that she loved him. For one Saturday, she promised to go out for lunch with him at the popular restaurant the next day.

She was at the bus stop first, waiting for him at the fixed time, which surprised him. When he arrived, she said to him: "Before going, I want to talk to you. We still have twenty minutes before our agreed time, and that is more than I shall take for what I have to say."

She trembled as she hung on his arm, and looked down, her cheeks pale, as she continued: "I do not want you to deceive me, and I shall not go out with you, unless you promise, unless you swear not to do—not to do anything that is at all morally improper." She said.

He did not know what to reply, for he was happy and disappointed at the same time. It was beginning to dawn on him that she grow up in a strictly, morally guarded home. He reasoned, 'how can? I should have preferred a little flirtation with her. This means that he would not be able to show love affection to her as much as he wanted; certainly, if he knew that her conduct was light.

As he did not say anything, she began to speak again in an agitated voice and with tears in her eyes. "If you do not promise to respect me altogether, I shall return home." And then he squeezed her arm tenderly and replied: "I promise, I will only do what you like." She then appeared relieved in mind, and asked, with a smile: "Do you really mean it?" And he looked into her eyes and replied: "I swear it"

"Now you may stop the bus," she said.

During the journey, they hardly spoke with each other, as the bus was full, and they felt shy in front of all those passengers. When they came down at the bus stop leading to the restaurant, they walked slowly, saying nothing to each other. Cassidy is a very shy guy and so is she. It just seems that they were both content to walk hand in hand, not saying a word, maybe taking their time to enjoy the environment. The sun, shone full on the sky, the leaves and the grass, seemed to be reflecting with joy in their hearts, and they went, hand in hand, along the road, looking at the cars as they drove by, and they walked on, brimming over with happiness, as if they were walking on air.

At last she said: "How foolish you must think I am!"

"Why?" he asked. "To come out like this, all alone with you, a stranger."

"Certainly not; it is quite normal."

"No, no; it is not normal for me. I do not wish to feel guilty of any stupid behavior, as you know this is how girls fall foolishly it problems. But if you only knew how boring life is: every day the same thing, every day of the month and every month of the year. I live alone with my mother, she have been sick for a long time and is always in pain. Because of that, she is hardly in a cheerful mood. I do the best I can, and try to be happy in spite of everything, but I do not always succeed. But, all the same, it was wrong of me to come alone to someone I don't know much, though you, I mean boys, always think they have nothing to lose."

By way of an answer, he kissed her passionately on the ear that was nearest to him, but she moved away from him immediately, almost getting offended and she bitterly complained: "Oh! Cassidy, after what you swore to me!" He apologized to her and assured her he won't do it again. And they both went into the restaurant.

The restaurant was a low house, buried under four enormous trees by the side of the road. Initially, the confusing rattling of some people seated at the nearby table, who were arguing aloud, made them unsettled; but, after taking a glass of wine, and some delicious meal with another glass of wine, they left, crossing the flyover nearby. Instead of going for the bus stop, they started off along the road, toward the layout nearby. Suddenly and for the first time he asked: "What-is your name?"

"Sasha."

"Sasha," he repeated, and said nothing more.

The girl picked some wild flower nearby and made them into a bunch, while he sang melodiously, like a child, whose longings have been satisfied. On their left is a shrub-covered slope close to the little stream nearby. Cassidy stopped motionless with astonishment: "Oh, look there!" he said.

The shrub had come to an end, and the whole slope was covered with lilac flower. It is a nice carpet of flowers stretched over the earth, reaching as far as the layout nearby, about a mile ahead. She also stood, surprised and delighted, and said: "Oh! how pretty!", They walked into the slop, admiring the beauty of nature from those beautiful, natural flower beds.

There was a narrow path beneath the only tree nearby, so they walked past it, and when they came to a small clearing, they sat down.

Swarms of flies were buzzing around them and making a continuous, gentle sound. The sun, the bright sun of a perfectly still day, shone over the slopes and from that flower bed, comes an exciting smell of fresh fragrance of scent.

They could hardly hear the noise of the busy street, even the horn of a heavy duty truck sounding from a little distant. They kept looking at each other's eyes and as if a magnet was placed between them; they moved closer to each other and embraced gently. Not conscious of what they are doing, they began to kiss, lying down on the grass. But she soon came to herself with the feeling of a great fear and confusion. She felt she would have been too loose, so she began to cry and sob with grief, her face buried in her hands.

He tried to console her, but she got up and start of home immediately; she kept saying, as she walked down very fast,: “My God! My God, how loose I am!”

He called out to her: “Sasha! Sasha! Please let us stop here.” But she would not listen. Her cheeks were red and her eyes hollow, and, as soon as they got to the bus stop, she left him without even saying goodby.

When he met her on the big bus, the next day, she appeared to be a changed person and look thinner, and she said to him: “I want to talk to you; we will get down at the traffic light.”

As soon as they were on the pavement, she said: “We must bid each other good-by; I cannot meet you again.”

“But why?” he asked.

“Because I cannot; I have over-stepped my bound, and I will not do so again.”

Then he begged her, tortured by his love, but she replied firmly: “No, I cannot, I cannot.” He, however, only grew all the more excited and promised to marry her, but she said again: “No,” and left him.

For one entire week, he did not see her. He could not manage to meet her, and, as he did not know her address, he thought that he had lost her altogether. On the ninth day, his doorbell rang, and on opening the door, behold!, Sasha was standing before him. She threw herself into his arms and did not resist any longer. And from then on, for three months, they were more than close friends. They were lovers.

Before the three months was over without any reason Cassidy started growing tired of her, forgetting to know that he who prays for the rain must prepare for the mud and that human fantasy is always devoid of responsibility at list makes it fun. One day, she whispered to him that she was pregnant. Immediately without further consideration he had one idea and wish: to break-up with her at all costs. But, however, he could not do that, not knowing how to begin, or what to say, full of anxiety through fear of the consequences of his rash indiscretion, he took a decisive step: one night he changed his place of residence and rented another apartment in another place far from where he lived; he bought a new mobile line, throw away his previous number, deleted his social media account and disappeared.

When Sasha came to see him after work as she used to do every day, she was shocked to meet an empty apartment without any furniture and without her husband to be anywhere in sight. The blow was so heavy and shocking to her that she did not make any attempt to look for the man who had abandoned her, but went home to her mother, threw herself at her mother's knees and confessed her misfortune to her. She was even discriminated by her employee who made up excuses when they found out within few months that she was pregnant. During this period she suffered heavily from financial problems and the struggle to take care of her sick mother. Few months after, she gave birth to a baby boy.

Years have passed, and Cassidy grew old and still not married, without him having much improvement in his life. He lived a dull, monotonous life of an office Chief servant, like a person stock in a time loop, without hope and future expectation. Every day he got up at the same time, went through the same streets, walk pass the same buildings, went through the same door, past the same porter, went into the same office, sat in the same chair, and did the same work. He was alone in the world, alone during the day, in the midst of his different colleagues, and alone at night in his bachelor's apartment. When his mother was alive, she have always nagged him about getting married but somehow the zeal or desire for it was not there. He seems to find it hard to fall in love with anybody, nor has he ever experienced a serious relationship, since he broke the vow to marry Sasha. It is as if he is suffering from the phobia of being committed or responsible for another person's welfare apart from himself.

Every Sunday he went to the Orbit Gardens and Park, (a happening recreation center in town) to watch the elegant people, cars and the pretty women, he always boast to his colleagues in the office about his escapades at 'Orbit Gardens and park' One fine Sunday morning, however, he went to another Amusement Park, where some women and care-givers usually bring their children for recreation, and suddenly, Cassidy Porter sighted a woman passing by, holding two children by the hand, a little boy of about ten and a little girl of four. It was her!

He walked another hundred yards opposite them and fell into a chair, choked with emotion. She saw him, but did not recognize him. When he recovered from the shock, after she have left the park with the children, he resolved to come back the next Sunday, wishing to see her again. She did come, but was already there before he arrived. She was sitting down, and the boy was standing by her side very quietly, while the little girl was making a sand dish beside her. It was her; it was certainly her, but she had the undoubtable appearance of a comfortable lady. She is richly dressed and looked graceful and dignified. He looked at her from a distance, for he did not venture to go near; but the little boy raised his head, and Cassidy felt himself trembling. It was his own son. There could be no doubt of that. And, as he looked at him, he thought he could recognize himself as he appeared in an old photograph taken years ago. He remained hidden behind a tree, waiting for her to go so that he could go.

He did not sleep that night. The thought of the child being his son tormented him the most. His son! Oh, if he could only have known, have been sure! But what can he do about it?

The following day, however, he started to investigate and found out where she used to live with her mother. He went to the house and asked about her. He was told that a neighbor, an honorable man of strict morals, had been touched by her distress and married her; he understood the sincere mistakes she had made, and still married her, and had even accepted the child, his, Cassidy's child, as his own.

He returned to the Amusement Park every Sunday, for there he always saw her, and each time he battled, an irresistible longing to hold his son in his arms, to cover him with kisses and to steal him, to carry him away.

He suffered horribly in his wretched isolation as an old bachelor, with nobody to care for him, and he also suffered heavy mental torture, made by paternal tenderness springing from remorse, longing and jealousy and from that need of loving one's own children which nature has implanted in all. At last, he was determined to make a desperate attempt.

One day he went to the park where he usually see her. He went up to her as she entered the park, standing in the middle of the path, pale and with trembling lips: "You do not recognize me." he said to her. She raised her eyes, looked at him, with deep terror in her eyes she shouted fearfully aloud, and in a desperate agitation, she quickly took the two children by the hand and rushed away, dragging them after her, while he went home and wept inconsolably.

Months passed without him seeing her again at the park. Indeed, he suffered day and night, for a sense of guilt and his paternal love tortured him. He would gladly die if that is what it takes to kiss his son; he would have performed any task, braved any danger, ventured anything just to look at his son's eyes and hold him or, at list be once again with the woman he had ever loved. He searched for her phone number or social media account but was not successful; he wrote to her, but she did not reply, and, after writing about twenty letters to her, he saw that there was no hope of altering her determination, and then he made a desperate resolution of writing to her husband, being quite prepared to receive a bullet from his pistol, if need be. His letter only consist of a few lines, as follows:

Sir,

You must have a perfect knowledge of my name and who I am, but I am so wretched, so overcome by misery that my only hope is in you, and, therefore, I wish to request you to grant me an audience of only five minutes.

Yours, faithfully

Cassidy Porter

The next day he received the reply:

Sir,

I shall expect you to-morrow, Tuesday, at five o'clock.

As he went up the staircase, Cassidy's heart beat so violently that he had to stop several times. There was a heavy and violent thumping noise in his heart, like that of a hammer on an anvil, and he had difficulty to control his breathing, and had to hold on to the banisters, in order not to fall.

He rang the bell on the third floor, and when a maid opened the door, he asked: "Does Mr. Dexter Shepherd live here?" "Yes sir, please come in." She replied.

They showed him into the drawing-room; where he stood alone waiting for Mr. Shepherd to show up, feeling disorientated, like somebody in the midst of a catastrophe, until a door opened and a man came in. He was tall and had the appearance of a serious and mean man. He wore a black frock coat and pointed to a chair with his finger. Cassidy sat down, and then said, with choking breath: "I don't know if you know my name you know—"

Mr. Shepherd interrupted him. "You don't need to tell me, mister, I know it. My wife has spoken to me about you." He spoke in a dignified tone of a respectable man who doesn't wish to insult the idiosyncrasies of his guest, and Cassidy continued,

"Well, Sir, I want to say this: I am dying of grief, of remorse, of shame, and I would like once, only once to hold the child." I have a letter which I wrote and signed myself. It says that if I am allowed to kiss the child just once, I will never again disturb you or your family again as long as I live, for I deserve whatever comes to me now. Here is the letter,", pulling it out of his pocket and placing it on the table before him.

Mr. Shepherd was shocked at first, not expecting what he was up to, but after some thoughts he took the letter, read it, got up and rang the bell. The maid came in, he said: "fetch Lewis here?" When she had gone out, they remained silent, not saying any word to each other as they had nothing more to say to one another, and waited. Then, suddenly, a little boy of ten rushed into the room and ran up to the man whom he believed to be his father, but he stopped when he saw the stranger, and Mr. Shepherd kissed him and said: "Now, go and kiss that gentleman, my dear." And the child went up to the stranger and looked at him. Cassidy had risen,0020 removed his hat which fell off his hand and stretched his hands to hold the boy-his biological son. He was ready to fall himself as he looked at his son, while Dexter Shepherd turned away, filled with emotion, and looked out of the window.

The child waited in surprise; but he picked up the hat and gave it to the stranger. Then Cassidy, taking the child up in his arms, began to kiss him wildly all over his face; on his eyes, his cheeks, his mouth, his hair; and the youngster, frightened at the shower of kisses, tried to avoid them, turned away his head, and pushed away the man's face with his little hands. But suddenly Cassidy put him down and cried: "Good-by! good-by!" And he rushed out of the room, not looking back.

So far he had kept his promise, and they never heard from him or know what happened to him till this very day that I am writing this down (it has been eight years from the day he saw his son).

The End.

Neglected Necessity

One day in the month of June, Master Zacharias' fishing-basket was so full of salmon-trout, about three o'clock in the afternoon, that the good man was unwilling to take any more; for, as an adage says: "We must leave some for tomorrow!" After washing the fishes in the stream and carefully covered them with field-sorrel to keep them fresh; after having wound up his line and bathed his hands and face; a sense of drowsiness took over him and he felt like taking a nap in the heather. The weather was so hot that he preferred to wait until the shadows lengthened before climbing the steep ascent of the little valley.

He took some bites from the biscuits he came with and took a sip from his plastic bottle of lemonade; he climbed down fifteen or twenty steps from the path and stretched himself on the moss-covered ground, under the shade of the pine-trees; his eyelids heavy with sleep.

About an hour, the whistle of a bird, which sounded strange to him woke the retired judge up. He sat up to look around, and to his surprise; the so-called bird was a young girl of seventeen or eighteen years of age; fresh, with rosy cheeks and vermilion lips, brown hair, which hung in two long tresses behind her. A short poppy-colored skirt, with a tightly laced bodice, completed her costume. She was rapidly descending the sandy path down the side of the stream, a basket poised on her head, and her arms, a little sunburned, but plump, were gracefully resting on her hips.

"Oh, what a charming bird; her whistles are so delightful and her pretty chin, round like a peach, is sweet to look upon."

Mr. Zacharias was filled with emotion—a rush of hot blood, which made his heart beat, as it did at twenty, coursed through his veins. Blushing, he arose to his feet.

"Good-day, pretty one!" he said.

The young girl stopped short—her big eyes brightened and looking at him, she recognized him (for who did not know the dear old Judge Zacharias in that part of the country?).

"Ah!" she said, with a bright smile, "it you Mr. Zacharias Seiler!"

The old man approached her—he tried to speak—but all he could do was to stammer a few unintelligible words, just like a very young man. His embarrassment was so great that he completely confused the young girl. At last, he managed to say,

"Where are you going through the forest at this hour, my dear child?"

She stretched out her hand and showed him, way at the end of the valley, a forester's house.

"I am returning to my father's house, the Corporal Yeri Foerster. You know him, without doubt, sir."

"Oh! you are the brave Yeri's daughter? Ah, and you ask if I know him? Of course, a very worthy man. Then you are little Charlotte, of whom he has often spoken to me when he came with his official reports?"

"Yes, sir I am; I have just come from the town and am returning home."

"That is a very pretty bunch of Alpine berries you have,'" exclaimed the old man.

She detached the bouquet from her belt and tendered it to him.

"If it would please you, sir Seiler."

Zacharias was touched.

"Yes, indeed," he said, "I will accept it, and I will accompany you home. I am anxious to see this brave Foerster again. He must be getting old by now."

"He is about your age, sir," said Charlotte innocently, "between fifty-five and sixty years of age."

This simple speech brought back the good man to his senses, and as he walked beside her, he became thoughtful.

What was he thinking of? Nobody could tell; but how many times, how many times has it happened that a brave and worthy man, who believed that he had fulfilled all his duties and have accomplished a lot in his life more than his pairs, and towards the end figured out that he has neglected the greatest, the most sacred, the most beautiful of all—that of love. And how it is so neglected that the worries of it came all of a sudden to start living just for it, like a teenager at a very matured age.

Soon Mr. Zacharias and Charlotte came to the turn of the valley where the path spanned a little pond by means of a rustic bridge, and led straight to the corporal's house. They could now see Yeri Foerster, his large felt hat decorated with a twig of heather, his calm eyes, his brown cheeks and grayish hair, seated on the stone bench near his doorway; two beautiful hunting dogs, with reddish-brown coats, lay at his feet, and the high vine arbor behind him rose to the peak of the gable roof.

The shadows on Romerstein were lengthening and the setting sun spread its purple fringe behind the high fir-trees on Alpnach.

The old corporal, whose eyes were as piercing as an eagle's, recognized the Judge Zacharias and his daughter from afar. He came toward them, lifting his felt hat respectfully.

“Welcome, Your Honour,” he said in the frank and cordial voice of a mountaineer; “what fortunate circumstance has procured me the honor of a visit?”

“Mr. Yeri,” replied the Judge, “I am behind time in your mountains. Have you a vacant corner at your table and a bed at the disposition of a friend?”

“Ah!” cried the corporal, “if there were but one bed in the house, should it not be at the service of the best, and most honored, of our ex-magistrates? Your Honour, what an honor you confer on Yeri Foerster’s humble home.”

“Christine, Christine! Your Honour Judge Zacharias Seiler wishes to sleep under our roof to-night.”

Then a little matured woman, her face wrinkled like a vine leaf, but still fresh and lively, her head crowned by a cap, appeared on the threshold and disappeared again, murmuring:

“What? Is it possible? The Judge Zacharias!”

“My good people,” said Mr. Zacharias, “truly you do me too much honor—I hope—”

“Your Honour, if you forget the favors you have done to others, they do remember them.”

Charlotte placed her basket on the table, feeling very proud at having been the means of bringing so distinguished a visitor to the house. She took out the sugar, the coffee and all the little household provisions which she had purchased in the town. And Zacharias, gazing at her pretty profile, felt himself agitated once more. His heart beat more quickly in his bosom and seemed to say to him: “This is love, Zacharias! This is love! This is love!”

To tell you the truth, my dear friends, Mr. Seiler, spent the evening with Mr. Forester, not concerned about the worries his house keeper Mrs. Therese is in because of his unusual absence. He promised to return before seven o’clock, to all his old habits of order and submission.

Picture to yourself the large room, the time-browned rafters of the ceiling, the windows opened on the silent valley, the round table in the middle of the room, covered with a white cloth, with red stripes running through it; the light from the electric bulb, bringing out more clearly the grave faces of Zacharias and Yeri, the rosy, young features of Charlotte, and Dame Christine, listening attentively at the conversation. Picture to yourself the soup-tureen, with a lovely flowered bowl, from which arose an appetizing aroma, the dish of trout garnished with parsley, the plates filled with fruits and little meal cakes as yellow as gold; then worthy Father Zacharias, handing first one and then the other of the plates of fruit and cakes to Charlotte, who lowered her eyes, frightened by the old man's compliments and tender speeches.

Yeri was quite puffed up at his praise, but Dame Christine said: "Ah, Your Honour! You are too good. You do not know how much trouble this little girl gives us, or how headstrong she is when she wants anything. You will spoil her with so many compliments."

To which Mr. Zacharias will reply:

"Dame Christine, you possess a treasure! Miss Charlotte merits all the qualities I have said of her."

Then Master Yeri, raising his glass, cried out: "Let us drink to the health of our good and venerated Judge Zacharias Seiler!"

The toast was drunk with joy.

Just then, the clock, in its hoarse voice, struck the hour of eleven. Out of doors there was the significant silence of the forest, the grasshopper's last cry, the vague murmur of the river. As the hour sounded, they rose, preparatory to retiring. How fresh and agile he felt! With what ardor had he had dared, would he not have pressed a kiss upon Charlotte's little hand! Oh, but he must not think of that now! Later on, perhaps!

"Come, Yeri my good friend," he said, "it is bedtime. Goodnight, and many thanks for your hospitality."

"At what hour do you wish to rise, sir?" asked Christine.

"Oh!" he replied, gazing at Charlotte. "I am an early bird. I do not feel my age, though perhaps you might not think so. I rise at five o'clock."

"Just like me, Your Honour," cried the Mr. Forester. I rise before daybreak; but I must confess it is tiresome most times—we are no longer young. Ha! Ha!"

"Bah! I have never allowed anything to bother me, my good friend Forester; I have never been more vigorous or more nimble."

And to prove his words, he ran briskly up the steep steps of the staircase. Really, Mr. Zacharias was no more than twenty years at that moment; but his twenty years lasted about twenty minutes, and once nestled in the large bed, with the covers drawn up to his chin and his handkerchief tied around his head, as a substitute for a nightcap, he said to himself,

"Sleep Zacharias! Sleep! You have great need of rest; you are very tired."

And the good man slept until nine o'clock. The forester, returning from his rounds, uneasy at his non-appearance, went up to his room and wished him a good morning. Then seeing the sun high in the heavens, hearing the birds warbling in the foliage, the Judge, ashamed of his boastfulness of the previous night, arose, and start to blame his prolonged slumbers on the fatigue of fishing and the length of the supper of the evening before.

"Ah, Your Honour," said the Mr. Forester, "it is perfectly natural; I would love dearly myself to sleep in the mornings, but I must always be on the go. What I want is a son-in-law, a sturdy youth to replace me; I would voluntarily give him my gun and my hunting pouch."

Zacharias could not restrain a feeling of great uneasiness at these words. He got up immediately, refreshed himself, dressed up, and descended in silence. Mrs. Forester was waiting with his breakfast; Charlotte had gone to the hayfield.

The breakfast was short, and Mr. Seiler, having thanked these good people for their hospitality, turned his face toward home; and this was the only time he remembered and became troubled, as he thought of the worry to which Mrs. Theresa had been subjected; yet he was not able to tear his hopes from his heart, nor the thousand charming illusions, which came to him like a latecomer in competition.

By Autumn he had fallen so into the habit of going to the forester's house that he was oftener there than at his own; and the Mr. Forester, not knowing to what love of fishing to attribute these visits, often found himself embarrassed at being obliged to refuse the numerous gifts which the worthy ex-magistrate begged him to accept in compensation for his daily hospitality.

Besides, Mr. Seiler wished to share all his occupations, following him in his rounds in the forest.

Yeri Foerster often shook his head, saying: "I never knew a more honest or better judge than Mr. Zacharias Seiler. When I used to bring my reports to him, formerly, he always praised me, and it is to him that I owe my raise to the rank of Head Forester. But," he added, "I am afraid the poor man is a little out of his head. Did he not help Charlotte in the hayfield, to the infinite amusement of the onlookers? Truly, Christine, it is not right; but then I don't know how to tell him that level is so much above us. Now he wants me to accept a pension from him—and such a pension—a monthly pension. And that silk dress he gave Charlotte on her birthday. Do young girls of her level wear such rich silk dresses in our valley? Is a silk dress the thing for a forester's daughter?"

"Leave him alone," said his wife. "He has been rich and in the limelight all his life and he now finds it new and fun to be like us, poor and unknown. He is contented with our little milk and meal. He likes to be with us; it is a change from his lonesome city life, with no one to talk to but his old governess; whilst our daughter is also found of him. He likes to talk to her. Who knows, but he may end by adopting her and leave her something in his will?"

Mr. Forester, not knowing what to say, shrugged his shoulders; his good judgment told him there was some mystery, but he never dreamed of suspecting the good man's craziness.

One fine morning, a station wagon slowly wended its way down the sides of the valley loaded with three casks of old wine. Of all the presents that could be given to him, this was the most acceptable, for Yeri Foerster loved, above everything else, a good glass of wine.

"That warms one up," he would say, laughing. And when he had tasted this wine, he could not help saying,

"Mr. Zacharias is really the best man in the world. Has he not filled my cellar for me? Charlotte, go and gather the prettiest flowers in the garden; cut all the roses and the jasmine, make them into a bouquet, and when he comes, you will present them to him yourself. Charlotte! Charlotte! Hurry up, here he comes with his long pole."

At this moment, the old man appeared, descending the hillside in the shade of the pines with a brisk step.

As far off as Yeri could make himself heard, he called out, his glass in his hand,

"Here is to the best man I know! Here is to our benefactor."

And Zacharias smiled. Dame Christine had already commenced preparations for dinner; a rabbit was turning at the spit and the savory aroma of the soup whetted Mr. Seiler's appetite.

The old Judge's eyes brightened when he saw Charlotte in her short poppy-colored skirt, her arms bare to the elbow, running here and there in the garden paths gathering the flowers, and when he saw her approaching him with her huge bouquet, which she humbly presented to him with downcast eyes.

"Your Honour, will you please accept this bouquet from your little friend Charlotte?"

A sudden blush overspread his venerable cheeks, and as she stooped to kiss his hand, he said,

"No, no, my dear child; accept rather from your old friend, your best friend, a more tender embrace."

He kissed both her burning cheeks. Mr. Forester, laughing heartily, cried out,

"Mr. Seiler, good friend, come and sit down under the acacia tree and drink some of your own wine. Ah, my wife is right when she calls you our benefactor."

Mr. Zacharias seated himself at the little round table, placing his pole behind him; Charlotte sat facing him. Yeri Foerster was on his right; then dinner was served and Mr. Seiler started to speak of his plans for the future.

He was wealthy and had also inherited a fine fortune from his parents. He wished to buy some few hundred acres of forest land in the valley, and build in the midst a forester's lodge. "We would always be together," he said, turning to Yeri Foerster, "sometimes you at my house, sometimes I at yours."

Christine gave her advice, and they chatted, planning now one thing, then another. Charlotte seemed perfectly contented, and Zacharias imagined that these simple people understood him.

Thus the time passed, and when night had fallen and they had drunk excess wine, and have eaten the rabbit and of Dame Christine's delicious soup. Mr. Seiler, happy and contented, full of joyous hope, ascended to his room, putting off until tomorrow his declaration, not doubting for a moment that his proposal will be rejected.

About this time of the year, the mountaineers from the surrounding hamlets usually descend from their mountains about one o'clock in the morning to commence the mowing of high grass in the valleys. One can hear their monotonous songs in the middle of the night keeping time for the circular movement of the scythes, the jingle of the cattle bells, and the young men's and girls' voices laughing afar in the silence of the night. It is a strange harmony, especially when the night is clear and there is a bright moon, and the heavy dew falling makes a pitter-patter on the leaves of the great forest trees.

Mr. Zacharias heard nothing of all this, for he was sleeping soundly; but the noise of a handful of peas being thrown against the window waked him suddenly. He listened and heard outside below his window, a "scit! scit!" so softly whispered that you might almost think it was the cry of some bird. Nevertheless, the good man's heart fluttered.

"What is that?" he cried.

After a few seconds' silence, a soft voice replied,

"Charlotte, Charlotte—it is me!"

Zacharias trembled; and as he listened with ears on the alert for each sound, the foliage on the trellis struck against the window and a figure climbed up quietly—oh so quietly—then stopped and stared into the room.

The old man, being indignant at this, rose and opened the window, upon which the stranger climbed through noiselessly.

"Do not be frightened, Charlotte," he said. "I have come to tell you some good news. My father will be here tomorrow."

He received no response for the reason that Zacharias was trying to light the lamp.

"Where are you, Charlotte?"

"Here I am," cried the old man, turning with a livid face and gazing fiercely at his rival.

The young man who stood before him was tall and slender, with large, frank, black eyes, brown cheeks, rosy lips, just covered with a little moustache, and a large brown felt hat, tilted a little to one side.

The apparition of Zacharias stunned him, motionless, as if riveted by a nail gun on that spot. But as the Judge was about to cry out, he exclaimed,

"In the name of God, do not call. I am no robber—I love Charlotte!"

"And—she—she?" stammered Zacharias.

"She loves me also! Oh, you need to have no fear if you are one of her relations. We were betrothed at the Easter feast. The fiancée of the Grindelwald and the Entilbach have the right to visit in the night. It is a custom of Unterwald. All the Swiss know that."

“Yeri Foerster—Yeri, Charlotte’s father, never told me.”

“No, he does not know of our betrothal yet,” said the other, in a lower tone of voice; “when I asked his permission last year, he told me to wait—that his daughter was still too young—we were betrothed secretly. Because I had not the Forester’s consent yet, I did not come in the night-time. This is the first time. I saw Charlotte in the town today; and both of us cannot wait any longer and i confessing all to my father, and he has promised to see Yeri tomorrow. Ah, Sir, I knew it would give such pleasure to Charlotte that I could not help coming to announce my good news.”

The poor old man fell back in his chair and covered his face with his hands. Oh, how he suffered! What bitter thoughts passed through his brain; what a sad awakening after so many sweet and joyous dreams.

And the young mountaineer was not a whit more comfortable, as he stood leaning against a corner of the wall, his arms crossed over his breast, and the following thoughts running through his head:

“If old Foerster, who does not know of our betrothal, finds me here, he will kill me without listening to one word of explanation. That is certain.”

And he gazed anxiously at the door, his ear on the alert for the least sound.

A few moments afterward, Zacharias lifting his head, as though awakening from a dream, asked him,

"What is your name?"

"Karl Imnant, sir."

"What is your business?"

"My father hopes to obtain the position of a forester around here for me."

There was a long silence, and Zacharias looked at the young man with an envious eye.

"And she loves you?" he asked in a broken voice.

"Oh, yes, sir; we love each other devotedly."

And Zacharias, letting his eyes fall on his thin legs and his hands wrinkled and veined, murmured:

"Yes, she ought to love him; he is young and handsome."

And his head fell on his breast again. All at once he arose, trembling in every limb, and opened the window.

"Young man, you have done very wrong; you will never know how much wrong you have really done.

You must obtain Mr. Foerster's consent—but go—go, you will hear from me soon."

The young mountaineer did not wait for a second invitation; with one bound, he jumped to the path below and disappeared behind the grand old trees.

"Poor, poor Zacharias," the old Judge murmured, "all your illusions are fled."

At seven o'clock, having regained his usual calmness of demeanor, he descended to the room below, where Charlotte, Dame Christine and Yeri were already sited waiting for him for breakfast. The old man, turning his eyes from the young girl, advanced to Mr. Forester, saying,

"My friend, I have a favor to ask of you. You know the son of the forester of the Grinderwald, do you not?"

"Karl Imnant, yes I do, sir!"

"Is he a worthy young man, and well behaved?"

"I think so, sir."

"Is he capable of succeeding his father?"

"Yes, he is twenty-one years old; he knows all about tree-clipping, which is the most necessary thing of all—he knows how to read and how to write; but that is not all; he also shows an understanding of things happening in the forest."

"Well, Master Yeri, I still have some influence in the Department of Forests and Rivers. This day fortnight, or three weeks at the latest, Karl Imnant shall be Assistant Forester of the Grinderwald, and I ask the hand of your daughter Charlotte for this brave young man."

At this request, Charlotte, who had blushed and trembled with fear, uttered a cry and fell back into her mother's arms.

Her father, looking at her severely, said: "What is the matter, Charlotte? Do you refuse?"

"Oh, no, no, father—no, it is what I want!"

"That is as it should be! As for myself, I would never refuse any request of you, Mr. Zacharias Seiler's! go and embrace your benefactor, Charlotte."

Charlotte ran toward him and the old man pressed her to his heart, gazing long and earnestly at her, with eyes filled with tears. Then, pleading business, he started home, with only a crust of bread in his basket for breakfast.

Fifteen days afterward, Karl Imnant received the appointment as a forester, taking his father's place. Eight days later, he and Charlotte were married.

The guests drank the rich old wine, so highly esteemed by Yeri Foerster, and which seemed to him was sent because of the feast.

Mr. Zacharias Seiler was not present that day at the wedding, being ill at home. Since then, he rarely goes fishing at the stream—but always at the other side of the town—toward the lake; at the other side of the mountain.

The End

The Adoption

In a certain small town, there were two houses that stood beside each other at the foot of a hill near a little stream resort. Two men and their families where the occupants of these houses both of them were best friends and they both earn their livelihood as factory works in cement factory nearby. Each family had four children.

These families were so close that their children go to the same school and play together at home, very close to their houses were hips of sand more than six feet high that is seemed to be abandoned or forgotten by the cement factory operators who dumped it there a long time ago, the whole troop of naughty children played and tumbled about on these hips of sand from morning till night. The two eldest were six years old, and the youngest were about fifteen months; the marriages, and afterward the births, having taken place nearly simultaneously in both families.

The two mothers could hardly distinguish their own children from the group, and as for the fathers, they were altogether at sea. The eight names danced in their heads; they were always getting them mixed up; and when they wished to call one child, the men often called up to three names before getting the right one.

The first of the two houses, as you came up from the bathing beach, was occupied by the Millers, who had two girls and two boys; the other house sheltered the Wilsons, who had one girl and three boys.

The families, not being rich, lived daily and frugally on a very simple and cheap diet. Their meals were almost the same things day after day with very little changes that even the children by impulse know what they will eat at seven o'clock in the morning, at noon, and then at six o'clock in the evening, the housewives usually get their families together to give them their meal, as the hen collect their flock of chicks. The children were seated, according to age, before the wooden table, which is varnished by ten years of consistent usage; the mouths of the youngest hardly reaching the level of the table. Before them is placed a bowl filled with the main condiment, and another bowl which is usually filled with soap or stew; and the entire line ate until they appeased their hunger. The mothers themselves fed the smallest.

A small pot of rice on Sunday was a feast for all; and the father on this day sat longer over the meal, repeating: "I wish we could have this every day."

One afternoon, in the month of August, a 4x4 car halted in front of the house, and a young woman, who was driving the car, said to the man sitting at her side:

"Oh, look at all those children, Henry! How pretty they are, tumbling about in the dust, like that!"

The man did not answer, accustomed to these outbursts of admiration, which were a pain and almost a reproach to him. The young woman continued,

"I must hug them! Oh, how I should like to have one of them—that one there—the little tiny one!"

Springing out from the car, she ran toward the children, took one of the two youngest—a Millers child—and lifting it up in her arms, she kissed him passionately on his dirty cheeks, on his tousled hair daubed with earth, and on his little hands, with which he fought vigorously, to get away from the caresses which displeased him.

Then she got into the car again and drove off at a lively trot. But she returned the following week, and seating herself on the ground, took the youngster in her arms, stuffed him with cakes; gave meat pie to all the others, and played with them like a young girl, while the husband waited patiently in the car.

She returned again; made the acquaintance of the parents, and reappeared every day with her pockets full of dainties and money.

Her name was Mrs. Stephanie Carter.

One morning, on arriving, her husband alighted with her, and without stopping to talk to the children, who now knew her well and always anticipate her coming, she entered the first house.

The wife of the occupant was busy washing their clothes while her husband was painting a corner of the room. They turned to look at their gust in surprise, brought forward chairs, and waited expectantly.

Then the woman, in a broken, trembling voice, began,

"My good people, I have come to see you, because I should like—I would like to take—your little boy with me—"

The country people, too bewildered to think, did not answer.

She recovered her breath, and continued: "We are alone, my husband and I. We would like to raise him. Are you willing?"

The farmer's wife began to understand. She asked:

"You want to take Allen from us? Oh, no indeed!"

Then Mr. Carter intervened:

"My wife has not made her meaning clear. We wish to adopt him, but he will always come to see you. If he turns out well, as there is every reason to expect, he will be our heir. If we, perhaps, later have children, he will share equally with them; but if he is not happy to stay with us, we would still take care of his tuition fees and when he comes of age, we shall deposit immediately a reasonable sum in his name, with a lawyer in his own bank account. As we have thought also of you, we would pay you an allowance, until your death, a pension of agreeable amount monthly. Do you understand me?"

The woman had stood up, furious.

"You want me to sell you Allen? Oh, no, that's not the sort of thing to ask of a mother! Oh, no! That would be an abomination!"

Her husband looked graved and seemed to be deliberating but said nothing; but approved of what his wife said with a continued nodding of his head.

Mrs. Stephanie Carters, in dismay, began to weep; turning to her husband, with a voice full of tears, the voice of a child used to having all its wishes gratified, she stammered:

"They will not do it, Henri. They will not do it."

Then he made a last attempt: "But, my friends think of the child's future, of his happiness, of—"

The latter's wife, however, exasperated, cut him short:

"It's all considered! we understood you very well! Get out of here and don't let me see you again—the idea of wanting to take away a child like that!"

Mrs. Stephanie Carters remembered that there were two children, quite a little, and she asked, through her tears, with the stubbornness of a headstrong and spoiled woman,

"But is the other little one not yours?"

Mr. Miller answered: "No, it is our neighbors'. You can go to them if you wish." Saying so, he stood up and motioned for them to leave. As the Carters leave, they could hear the indignant resounded voice of the wife.

The Wilsons were at the table, picking slices of bread which they parsimoniously spread with a little rancid butter.

Mr. Carter recommenced his proposals, but this time with more insinuations, more oratorical precautions, more shrewdness.

The two village people shook their heads, in sign of refusal, but when they learned that they were to have a pension of reasonable amount a month, they considered the matter, consulting one another by glances, much disturbed. They kept silent for a long time, tortured, hesitating. At last the woman asked: "What do you say to it, man?" In a weighty tone he said: "I say that it's not to be despised."

Mrs. Stephanie Carters, trembling with anguish, spoke of the future of their child, of his happiness, and of the money which he could give them later.

The humbled Wilsons asked: "This monthly pension will it be promised before a lawyer?"

Mrs. Stephanie Carters responded: "Why, certainly, beginning with tomorrow."

The woman, who was thinking it over, continued,

“A pension of that amount a month is not enough to pay for depriving us of the child. That child would be working in a few years; we must have something added to it."

Tapping her foot with impatience, Mrs. Stephanie Carter granted it at once, and, as she wished to carry off the child with her, she gave them some cash immediately as a gift, while her husband drew up a paper and called their lawyer immediately in case the Wilsons change their minds if they delay. The young Mrs. Carter joyfully carried off the howling brat, as one carries away a wished-for knick-knack from a shop.

The Millers, from their door, watched her departure, silently and soberly, perhaps regretting their refusal.

Nothing much was heard of little John Wilson. The parents went to the bank every month to collect their pension. They had quarreled with their neighbors because Mrs. Miller grossly insulted them, continually repeating from door to door that they are cold-blooded to sell their child; that it was disgusting, disgraceful, she consistently try to make their life miserable. Sometimes she would take her child Allen in her arms, pretentiously exclaiming, as if he understood,

"I didn't sell you, I didn't! My little one, I didn't sell you! I'm not rich, but I don't sell my children!”

The Wilsons lived comfortably, thanks to the pension, which was gradually increased by the Carters with time. That was also the cause of the unquenchable fury of the

Millers, who had remained miserably poor. Their eldest went away to serve his time in the army; Allen alone remained to work in the cement factory with his old father, to support the mother and two younger sisters.

He had reached twenty-one years when, one morning, a brilliant car stopped before the two houses. A young man, with a gold-chain watch, got out, giving his hand to an aged, white-haired lady. The old lady said to him: "It is there, my child, at the second house." And he entered the house of the Wilsons as though at home.

The old mother was washing her clothes; the infirm father slumbered in his chair. Both raised their heads, and the young man said,

"Good-morning, Papa; good-morning, Mamma!"

They both stood up, frightened! In excitement, the Mrs. Wilson dropped her soap into the water, and stammered,

"Is it you, my child? Is it you, my child?"

He took her in his arms and hugged her, repeating: "Good-morning, mamma," While Mr. Wilson said in a trembling voice, and calm tone which he never lost: "Here you are, back again, John," as if he had just seen him a month ago.

When they had got to know one another again, the parents wished to take their boy out and show him off in the neighborhood, since they have been greatly ridiculed by some people. They took him to the Mayor, to the owners of the cement factory, to the parish priest, in fact everywhere they can think of.

Allen, standing on the threshold of his their house, watched him pass. In the evening, at supper, he said to his old parents: "You must have been stupid to let the Wilsons' boy be taken."

The mother answered, obstinately: "I wouldn't sell my child."

The father remained silent. The son continued,

"It is unfortunate to be sacrificed like that."

Then Mr. Miller, in an angry tone, said,

"Are you going to reproach us for having kept you?" And the young man said, brutally,

"Yes, I reproach you for having been such fools. Parents like you make the misfortune of their children. You deserve that. I should leave you."

The old woman wept over her plate. She moaned, as she tried to eat her food, half of which she spilled: "One may kill one's self to bring up children, how can we be sure she didn't intend to use you for something creepy"

Then the boy said, roughly: "creepy! how can you talk of that when the arrangement is made through a known layer? I'd rather not have been born than be what I am. When I saw John, my heart stood still. I said to myself: 'See what I should have been now!'" He got up: "See here, I feel that I would do better not to stay here, because I would throw it up to you from morning till night, and I would make your life miserable. I'll never forgive you for that!"

The two old people were silent, downcast, in tears.

He continued: "No, the thought of that would be too much. I'd rather look for a living somewhere else."

He opened the door. A sound of voices came in at the door. The Wilsons were celebrating the return of their child.

John late told his biological parents that Mrs. Stephanie Carters, his foster mother, also had children of her own: a boy and a girl whom he knows as his younger siblings. After some days, he went back to his foster parent but visits his biological parents often.

The End

The Gold Digger

The other day I went to a wedding... But no! I would rather tell you what brought about the wedding. The wedding was superb. I liked it immensely. But the other incident was still contemptible. I don't know why it is that the sight of the wedding reminded me of the Christmas tree. This is the way it happened:

Exactly five years ago, on New Year's Eve, I was invited to a children's party by a man high up in the business world, who had his connections, his circle of acquaintances. So it seemed as though the children's party was merely a pretext for the parents to come together and discuss matters of interest to themselves, quite freely and casually.

I was more of an outsider, not a close friend of the family and, as I had not much acquaintances to talk to, I was able to spend the evening independently of the others. There was another man present who, like me, had just stumbled upon this affair of domestic bliss. He was the first to attract my attention. His appearance was not that of a man of class or a man from a rich family. He was tall, rather thin, very serious, and well dressed. Apparently, he had no heart for the family festivities. The instant he went off into a corner by himself, the smile disappeared from his face, and his thick dark brows knitted into a frown. He knew no one except the host and showed every sign of being bored to death, though he sustained it bravely and acted as if he enjoyed everything to the end. Later I learned that he was from the countryside, had come to the city on some important, brain-racking business, had brought a letter of recommendation to our host. It was merely out of politeness that he had invited him to the children's party.

They did not chart with him; they did not offer him cigars. No one entered into the conversation with him. Possibly they recognised the bird by its feathers from a distance. Thus, the man, not knowing what to do with his hands, was compelled to spend the evening stroking his moustache. His moustache was really fine, but he stroked them so diligently that one got the feeling that the moustache had come into the world to be stroked into whiskers.

There was another guest who interested me. But he was of quite a different order. He was a very important person (VIP). They called him Julian Mastakovich. At first glance, one could easily guess that he was an honoured guest and of the same class as the host, but not of the same as the gentleman of the whiskers. The host and hostess said no end of kind things to him, were most attentive, wining him, hovering over him, bringing guests up to be introduced, but never leading him to anyone else. I noticed tears glisten in our host's eyes when Julian Mastakovich remarked that this was the most pleasant evening he would have ever spent. Somehow I began to feel uncomfortable in this very important guest's presence. So, after amusing myself with the children, five of whom, remarkably well-fed and richly dressed, were our host's, I went into a little sitting-room, entirely unoccupied, and seated myself at the end that was a conservatoire and took up almost half the room.

The children were charming. They absolutely did not resemble their parents, both in appearance and in character. Upon all the efforts of their mothers and servants to put the children under control, in a very short period they had striped the Christmas tree down to the very last sweet and had already succeeded in breaking half of their toys before they even found out which belonged to whom.

One of them was a particularly handsome little boy, dark-eyed, curly-haired, who stubbornly persisted in aiming at me with his plastic gun. But the child that attracted the greatest attention was his sister, a girl of about twelve or so, lovely as a Cupid. She was quiet and thoughtful, with large, dreamy eyes. The children had somehow annoyed her, and she left them and walked into the same room that I had withdrawn into. There she seated herself with her doll in a corner.

"Her father is an immensely wealthy businessman," the guests informed each other in tones of awe. "Three million set aside for her dowry already." As you may know when someone is rich he would like to tell you how valuable and important the traditions of their forefathers is and how it is beneficial to keep it but when one is poor the struggle to survive have no further room for the luggage of tradition. Having said this, you must know that most people of affluence still place bride price on the heads of their daughters. This usually guarantees early marriage and sometimes a potential suitor (most times not of the girl's choice but of the parents).

As I turned to look at the group from which I heard this news item issuing, my glance met Julian Mastakovich's. He stood listening to the insipid chatter with an attitude of concentrated attention, with his hands behind his back and his head inclined to one side.

All the while, I was quite lost in wonder of the shrewdness our host displayed in the dispensing of the gifts. The little girl who was gossiped to have a dowry of three million received the most expensive doll, and the rest of the gifts were graded in value according to the diminishing scale of the parents' stations in life. The last child, a tiny boy of ten, thin, red-haired, freckled, came into possession of a small book of nature stories without illustrations. He was the housemaid's child. She was a poor widow, and her little boy, clad in a mercifully looking jacket, looked thoroughly crushed and intimidated. He took the book of nature stories and circled slowly about the other children's toys. He would have given anything to play with them. But he did not dare to. You could tell he already knew his place.

I like to observe children. It is fascinating to watch the individuality in them struggling for self-affirmation. I could see that the other children's gifts had tremendously charmed the red-haired boy, especially a toy theatre, in which he was so anxious to take a part, being very brainy he resolved to fawn upon the other children. He smiled and began to play with them. His one and only apple he handed over to a puffy bully looking kid whose pockets were already crammed with sweets, and he even carried another youngster pickback—all simply that he might be allowed to stay with the theatre.

But in a few moments, another bully, a bit older than him, felt offended by him for no reason, fell on him and start to strike him with his fist. He did not dare even to cry. His mother came and told him to leave off interfering with the other children's games, and he crept away to the same room the little girl and I were in. She let him sit down beside her, and the two set themselves busy dressing the expensive doll.

Almost half an hour passed, and I was nearly dozing off, as I sat there in the conservatory, half listening to the chatter of the red-haired boy and the dowered beauty, when Julian Mastakovich entered suddenly. He had slipped out of the drawing-room under cover of a noisy scene among the children. From my secluded corner, it had not escaped my notice that a few moments before he had been eagerly conversing with the rich girl's father, to whom he had only just been introduced.

He stood still for a while, reflecting and mumbling to himself, as if counting something on his fingers.

"Three million—three million—eleven—twelve—thirteen—sixteen—in five years! Let's say four per cent—

five times twelve—sixty, and on these sixty——. Let us assume that in five years it will amount to—well, four million. Hm—hm! But the shrewd old fox isn't likely to be satisfied with four per cent. He gets eight or even ten, perhaps. Let's suppose five million, five million, at least, that's for sure. Anything above that form interest—hm—"

He blew his nose and was about to leave the room when he noticed the dowered beauty and stood still. I was behind the plants, so he didn't notice me. He seemed to me to be quivering with excitement. It must have been his calculations that upset him so. He rubbed his hands and danced from place to place, and kept getting more and more excited. Finally, however, he conquered his emotions and came to a standstill. He cast a determined look at the future bride and wanted to move toward her, but glanced about first. Then, as if with a guilty conscience, he stepped over to the child on tip-toe, smiling, and bent down and kissed her head.

His coming was so unexpected that she uttered a shriek of alarm.

"What are you doing here, dear child?" he whispered, looking around and pinching her cheek.

"We're playing."

"What, with him?" said Julian Mastakovich with a look of disgust at the maid's child. "You should go into the living-room, boy," he said to him.

The boy remained silent and looked up at the man with wide-open eyes. Julian Mastakovich glanced round again cautiously and bent down over the girl.

"What have you got, a doll, my dear?"

"Yes, sir." The child quailed a little, and her brow wrinkled.

"A doll? And do you know, my dear, what dolls are made of?"

"No, sir," she said weakly, and lowered her head.

"Out of plastics and rags, my dear. You, boy, you go back to the living-room, to the children," said Julian Mastakovich, looking at the boy angrily.

The two children frowned. They caught hold of each other and would not part.

"And do you know why they gave you the doll?" asked Julian Mastakovich, dropping his voice lower and lower.

"No."

"Because you were a good, very good little girl the whole week."

Saying which, Julian Mastakovich was seized with a fit of excitement. He looked round and said in a tone faint, almost inaudible with excitement and impatience,

“If I come to visit your parents, will you love me, my dear?”

He tried to kiss the sweet little creature, but the red-haired boy saw that she was on the verge of tears, and he caught her hand and start to howl in sympathy. That enraged the Julian Mastakovich.

“Go away! Go away! Go back to the other room, to your playmates.”

“I don’t want him to. I don’t want him to! You go away!” cried the girl. “Live him alone! Live him alone!” She was almost weeping.

There was a sound of footsteps in the doorway. Julian Mastakovich stood up instantly and straightened up his nice attire. The red-haired boy was even more alarmed at the footsteps. He let go the girl’s hand, sidled along the wall, and escaped through the living-room into the dining-room.

Not to attract attention, Julian Mastakovich also made for the dining-room. He was red as a lobster. The sight of his face in a mirror seemed to embarrass him. Presumably he was annoyed at his own fervidness. and impatience. Without due respect to his importance and dignity, his calculations had lured and pricked him to the greedy eagerness of a child, who makes straight for his object—though this was still an assumption and dreams, not as yet a reality; it only would be so in five years' time. I followed the worthy man into the dining-room, where I witnessed a remarkable play.

Julian Mastakovich, all flushed with anger, venomous in his looks, began to threaten the red-haired boy. The red-haired boy retreated farther and farther until there was no place left for him to retreat to, and he did not know where to turn in his fright.

"Get out of here! What are you doing here? Get out, I say, you good-for-nothing! Stealing fruit, are you? Oh, so, stealing fruit! Get out, you freckle face, go to your likes!"

The frightened child, as a last desperate resort, crawled quickly under the table. His persecutor, completely infuriated, pulled out his large linen handkerchief and used it as a lash to drive the boy out of his position.

Here I must remark that Julian Mastakovich was a somewhat obese man, heavy, well-fed, puffy-cheeked, with a paunch and ankles as round as nuts. He started sweating, puffed and panted. So strong was his dislike (or was his jealousy) of the child that he actually continue to harass the small boy like a madman.

I laughed out loud and heartily. Julian Mastakovich turned. He was utterly shocked and confused and for a moment start to recollect his faculties, and quite oblivious beginning to consider his immense importance. At that moment, our host appeared in the doorway opposite. The boy crawled out from under the table and wiped his knees and elbows. Julian Mastakovich hastened to pick up his handkerchief, which had fallen on the ground when my laughter thunder struck him. Our host looked at the three of us rather suspiciously. But, like a man who knows the world and can readily adjust himself, he seized upon the opportunity to lay hold of his very valuable guest and get what he wanted out of him.

“Here’s the boy I was talking to you about,” he said, indicating the red-haired child. “I took the liberty of presuming on your goodness on his behalf.”

“Oh,” replied Julian Mastakovich, still trying to recollect himself.

“He’s my maid’s son,” our host continued in a beseeching tone. “She’s a poor creature, the widow of an honest public servant. That’s why, if it were possible for you—”

“Impossible, impossible!” Julian Mastakovich cried hastily. “You must excuse me, Philip Alexeyevich. I really cannot. I’ve made inquiries. There are no vacancies, and there is a waiting list of ten who have a greater right—I’m sorry.”

“Too bad,” said our host. “He’s a quiet, unobtrusive child.”

“A very naughty little rascal, I should say,” said Julian Mastakovich, wryly. “Go away, boy. Why are you here still? Be off with you to the other children.”

Unable to control himself, he gave me a sidelong glance. Nor could I control myself. I laughed straight in his face. He turned away and asked our host, in tones quite audible to me, who that odd young fellow was (referring to me). They whispered to each other and left the room, disregarding me.

I shook with laughter. Then I, too, went to the living-room. There, the great Julian Mastakovich, already surrounded by the fathers and mothers and the host and the hostess, had begun to talk eagerly with a lady to whom he had just been introduced. The lady held the rich little girl's hand. Julian Mastakovich went into fulsome praise for the mother, who listened scarcely able to restrain tears of joy, while the father showed his delight with a gratified smile.

The joy was contagious. Everybody shared in it. Even the children were obliged to stop playing so as not to disturb the conversation. The atmosphere was surcharged with awe. I heard the mother of the important little girl, touched to her profoundest depths, ask Julian Mastakovich in the choicest language of courtesy, whether he would honour them by coming to see them. I heard Julian Mastakovich accept the invitation with genuine emotion and enthusiasm. Then the guests scattered decorously to different parts of the room, and I heard them, with veneration in their tones, praise the businessman, the businessman's wife, the businessman's daughter, and, especially, Julian Mastakovich.

In other to amuse myself and to rattle his nerves a little "Is he married?" I asked out loud of an acquaintance of mine standing beside Julian Mastakovich.

Julian Mastakovich gave me a venomous look.

"No," answered my acquaintance, profoundly shocked by my—intentional—indiscretion.

Not long ago I passed the Church of——. I was struck by the concourse of people gathered there to witness a wedding. It was a dreary day. A drizzling rain was beginning to come down. I made my way through the throng into the church. The bridegroom was a round, well-fed, pot-bellied little man, very much dressed up. He ran and fussed about and gave orders and arranged things. Finally, word was passed that the bride was coming. I pushed through the crowd, and I beheld a marvellous beauty whose first spring was scarcely commencing. But the beauty was pale and sad. She looked distracted. It seemed to me even that her eyes were red from recent weeping. The classic severity of every line of her face imparted a peculiar significance and solemnity to her beauty. But through that severity and solemnity, through the sadness, shone the innocence of a child. There was something inexpressibly naïve, unsettled and young in her features, which, without words, seemed to plead for mercy.

They said she was just eighteen years old. I looked at the bridegroom carefully. Suddenly our eyes meet and I recognised Julian Mastakovich, he too seems to remember me and flashed a venomous look at me. I had not seen him again in all those five years. Then I looked at the bride again.—Good God! I made my way, as quickly as I could, out of the church. I heard gossiping in the crowd about the bride's wealth—about her dowry of five million—so and so much for pocket money.

"Then his calculations were correct," I thought, as I pressed out into the street.

The End

Angel in Disguise

There was a woman in a certain village that was known for her unrestricted, licentious lifestyle. One day Idleness, moral weakness, and excessive indulgence of bodily appetites did their miserable work, in a drunken fit, she slipped and rolled down from the star case of her own house and was mortally injured after battling for life for some minutes she died in the presence of her frightened little children. The dead mother lay cold and still in the face of her terrified children, who could do nothing but scream and cry for their beloved to wake-up.

Death touches the spring of our common humanity. This woman had been hated, mocked, ridiculed, scoffed at, and angrily disgraced by nearly every man, woman, and children in the village even by those who patronize her secretly in the dark hours; but now, as the fact of her death was passed from lip to lip, in subdued tones, pity took the place of anger; and sorrow took the place of condemnation. Neighbors went hastily to the old dilapidated and abandoned house, in which she had secured as a home for herself and her children against the cold winter and summer heat: some with grave-clothes for a decent interment of the body; and some with food for the starving three children. Of these three children, the oldest is John: a boy of twelve, who is strong enough to survive on his own. Daisy, the second child, is between ten and eleven, is a bright, active girl, out of whom something clever might be made, if in good hands; but poor little Clara, the youngest, was hopelessly sickly. Two years ago, she fell from a window and injured her spinal cord, and she had not been able to leave her bed since, except when lifted in the arms of her mother.

"What is to be done with the children?" That was the chief question now. No relative of her has ever been known or seen. The dead mother would go underground and be forever beyond all care or concern of the villagers. But the children must not be left to starve. After considering the matter, and talking it over with his wife, the farmer George said that he would take John, and do well by him, now that his mother was out of the way; and Mrs. Hudson, who had been looking out for a young girl, concluded that it would be charitable for her to take Daisy to live with her, even though she was too young to be of much for her, but she can help out on domestic work.

"She could do much better, I know," said Mrs. Hudson; "but as no one seems inclined to take her, I must act from a sense of duty, expect to have trouble with the child; for she's an undisciplined thing, used to having her own way."

But no one said "I'll take Clara." Pitying glances were cast on her wan and wasted form and thoughts were troubled on her account. Mothers brought some clothes and, removing her soiled and ragged clothes, dressed her in clean attire. The sad eyes and patient face of the little one touched many hearts and even knocked at them for entrance. But none opened to take her in. Who wanted a bed-ridden child?

"Take her to the Orphanage," said a rough man, of whom the question "What's to be done with Clara?" was asked. "Nobody's going to be bothered with her." he said.

"The Orphanage is very far here and will be a sad place for a sick and helpless child," answered someone.

"For your child or mine," said the other, lightly speaking; "but for this brat it will prove a blessed change, she will be kept clean, have healthy food, and be attended to by a doctor, which is a major improvement of her past condition."

There was a reason for that, but still it wasn't satisfying. The day following, the villagers came together, though little in number, to bury the dead. No one seemed to be committed or care for the proper burial of the late woman. Farmer George, after the coffin was taken out and buried, placed John in his pickup van and drove away, satisfied that he had done his part.

Mrs. Hudson spoke to Daisy with a hurried air, "Bid your sister good-by," and drew the tearful children apart before scarcely their lips had touched in a sobbing farewell. Hastily others went out, some glancing at Clara, and some resolutely refraining from a look, until all had gone. She was alone! Just beyond the compound, Gabriel Nolan, the carpenter, paused, and said to the blacksmith's wife, who was hastening off with the rest,

"It's a cruel thing to leave her here."

"Then take her to the orphanage: she'll have to go there," answered the blacksmith's wife, springing away, and leaving Gabriel behind.

For a little while, the man stood with a puzzled air; then he turned back and went into the hovel again. Clara, with painful effort, had raised herself to an upright position and was sitting on the bed, straining her eyes upon the door through which all had just departed. A vague terror had come into her thin white face.

“O, uncle. Gabriel!" she cried out, catching her suspended breath, "don't leave me here all alone!”

Though rough outwardly, Gabriel Nolan, the carpenter, had a heart, and it was very tender in some places. He liked children, and was pleased to have them come to his shop, where furniture and doors were made. He makes toys for the village children without collecting a cent from them.

"No, dear," he answered, in a kind voice, going to the bed, and stooping down over the child, "You shall not be left here alone." Then he wrapped her with the gentleness almost of a woman, in the clean bedclothes which some neighbor had brought; and, lifting her in his strong arms, bore her out into the air and across the field that lay between the hovel and his home.

Now, Gabriel Nolan's wife, who happened to be childless, was not a woman of good temper, nor does she believe in sacrificing for others, and Gabriel had well-grounded knowledge that his wife will not give a damn of accepting the helpless child in their house. Mrs. Gabriel saw him approaching from the window, and with ruffling feathers, met him a few steps from the door, as he opened the compound gate, and came in. He carried the child like a precious burden, and he felt it to be so. As his arms held the sick child to his breast, a sphere of tenderness went out from her and penetrated his feelings. A bond had already corded itself around them both, and love was springing into life.

"What have you there?" sharply questioned Mrs. Gabriel.

Gabriel felt the fear of the child as she heard the harsh voice of Mrs. Gabriel and shrink against him in fear of his wife's voice. He did not reply, except by a look that was pleading and cautionary. He managed to say, under his breath, "Wait a moment for explanations, and be gentle;" and, passing in, carried Clara to the small chamber on the first floor, and laid her on a bed. Then, stepping back, he shut the door, and stood face to face with his vinegar-tempered wife in the passage-way.

"You haven't brought home that sick brat!" Anger and astonishment were in the tones of Mrs. Gabriel Nolan; her face was in a flame.

"I think women's hearts are sometimes very hard," said Gabriel. Usually Gabriel Nolan got out of his wife's way, or kept rigidly silent and non-combative when she fired up on any subject; it was with some surprise, therefore, that she now encountered a firmly set countenance and a resolute pair of eyes.

"Women's hearts are not half as hard as men's!"

Gabriel saw, by a quick intuition, that his resolute manner had impressed his wife and he answered quickly, and with real indignation, "Be that as it may, every woman at the funeral turned her eyes steadily from the sick child's face, and when the undertaker's went off with her dead mother, everybody hurried away, and left her alone in that ruined house, she was left to her fate, imposed on her by nature, and not of her own doing, to die there alone."

"Where were John and Daisy?" asked his wife, Mrs. Nolan.

“George the Farmer tossed John into his pickup van and drove off. Daisy went home with Mrs. Hudson; but nobody wanted the poor sick one. 'Send her to the orphanage,' was the cry.”

"Why didn't you let her go, then? What did you bring her here for?"

"She can't walk to the orphanage," said Gabriel; "somebody's arms must carry her, and mine are strong enough for that task."

"Then why didn't you keep on? Why did you stop here?" demanded the wife.

"Because I'm not apt to go on fools' errands. The orphanage is not close from here as you well know and besides, the Guardians must first be seen, and a permit obtained."

There was no gainsaying this.

"When will you see the Guardians?" was asked with irrepressible impatience.

"Tomorrow."

"Why put it off till tomorrow? Go at once for the permit and get the whole thing off of your hands tonight."

"Jane," said the carpenter, with all seriousness and tenacity of tone that greatly subdued his wife, "I do read the Bible sometimes, and find much said about little children. How the Savior rebuked the disciples who would not receive them; how he took them up in his arms, and blessed them; and how he said that 'whosoever gave them even a cup of cold water should not go unrewarded.' Now, it is a small thing for us to keep this poor motherless little one for a single night; to be kind to her for a single night; to make her life comfortable for a single night."

The voice of the strong, rough man shook, and he turned his head away, so that the moisture in his eyes might not be seen. Mrs. Gabriel did not answer, but a soft feeling crept into her heart.

"Look at her kindly, Jane; speak to her kindly," said Gabriel. "Think of her dead mother, and the loneliness, the pain, the sorrow that she must be in, right now, it is overwhelming for her age, none of us here had such an experience when we were her age!" The softness of his heart gave unwonted eloquence to his lips.

Mrs. Gabriel did not reply, but now turned towards the little chamber where her husband had kept Clara; and, pushing open the door, went quietly in. Gabriel did not follow; he saw that her state had changed and felt that it would be best to leave her alone with the child. So he went to his shop, which stood near the house, and worked until dusky. Only evening released him from labor.

On his way home from work, the bright light shining through the little room windows was the first thing that attracted Gabriel's attention on turning towards his house: it was a good omen. The path led him by these windows and, when opposite, he could not help pausing to peeping in. It was now dark enough outside to shield him from observation. Clara lay a little raised on the pillow with the light shining full upon her face. Mrs. Gabriel was sitting by the bed, talking to the child; but her back was towards the window, so that her countenance was not seen. From Clara's face, Gabriel read the atmosphere of their interaction. He saw that her eyes were intently fixed upon his wife; that now and then a few words came, as if in answers from her lips; also her expression was sad and tender; but he saw nothing of bitterness or pain. He drew a deep breath as a sign of relief, as he felt a weight lifted from his heart.

On entering, Gabriel did not go immediately to the little chamber. His heavy footsteps in the kitchen brought his wife's attention, and she hurried out from the room where she had been with Clara. Gabriel thought it best not to refer to the child, nor to show any concern in regard to her.

"How soon will dinner be ready?" he asked.

"Almost ready," answered Mrs. Gabriel, as she start to bustle about in other to get it ready. There was no harshness in her voice.

After washing off his hands and face the dust and soil of work, Gabriel left the kitchen and went to the little bedroom. A pair of large bright eyes looked up at him from the white soft bed; looked at him tenderly, gratefully, pleadingly. How his heart swelled in his bosom! With a faster motion came his heart-beats! Gabriel sat down, and for the first time, examining the thin face carefully under the bright light, he noticed how innocently beautiful it was, and full of a childish sweetness but pains had not allowed it to blossom, to its fullness.

"Your name is Clara?" he said, as he sat down and took her soft little hand in his.

"Yes, sir." Her voice struck a chord that quivered in a low strain of music.

"Have you been sick long?"

"Yes, sir." What a sweet patience was in her tone!

"Has the doctor been to see you?"

"He used to come."

"But not lately?"

"No, sir."

"Have you any pain?"

"Sometimes, but not now."

"When last did you experience pain?"

"This morning my side ached, and my back hurt when you carried me."

"It hurts you to be lifted or moved about?"

"Yes, sir."

"Your side doesn't ache now?"

"No, sir."

"Does it ache a great deal?"

"Yes, sir; but it hasn't ached since I've been on this soft bed."

"The soft bed feels good."

"O, yes, sir—so good!" What a satisfaction, mingled with gratitude, was in her voice!

"Dinner is ready," said Mrs. Gabriel, looking into the room a little while afterwards.

Gabriel glanced from his wife's face to that of Clara; she understood him and answered,

"She can wait until we are done; then I will bring her something to eat." There was an improvement in the indifference shown by Mrs. Gabriel, but her husband had seen her through the window, and understood that she was just pretending to be bitter. Gabriel waited, after sitting down at the table, for his wife to introduce the subject uppermost in both of their thoughts; but she kept silent on that theme for many minutes, and he maintained a little reserve. At last she said, abruptly,

"What are you going to do with that child?"

"I thought you understood me that she was to go to the orphanage," replied Gabriel, as if surprised at her question.

Mrs. Gabriel looked rather strangely at her husband for some moments, and then dropped her eyes. The subject was not again referred to during the meal. When they finished their meal, Mrs. Gabriel toasted some slice of bread and softened it with milk and butter; adding to this a cup of tea, she took them to Clara, and held the small saucer, on which she had placed them, while the hungry child ate with every sign of pleasure.

"Do you like it?" asked Mrs. Nolan, seeing with what a keen relish the food was taken.

The child paused with the cup in her hand, and answered with a look of gratitude that awoke a maternal feeling in her which she have longed for a long time but had been slumbering in her heart for half a score of years.

"We'll keep her a day or two longer; she is so weak and helpless," said Mrs. Gabriel Nolan, in answer to her husband's remark, at breakfast-time on the next morning, that he must go and see the Guardians of the orphanage about Clara.

"Won't it bother you so much?" said Gabriel.

"I won't mind that for a day or two. Poor thing!"

Gabriel did not see the Guardians of the orphanage on that day, or on the next, nor on the day following. In fact, he never saw them at all on Clara's account, for in less than a week Mrs. Gabriel Nolan did not talk about the orphanage anymore. There was this delight which she derived from bathing and charting with Clara.

What light and blessing did that sick and helpless child brought to the home of Gabriel Nolan, the poor carpenter! Before her coming into that home, it had been emotionally dark, and cold, and unhappy for a long time just because his wife had nothing to love and care for besides herself. And so, she became sore, irritable, ill-tempered, and self-afflicting in the desolation of her woman's nature. Now the sweetness of that sick child, looking ever to her in love, patience, and gratitude, was as honey to her soul, and she carried her in her heart as well as in her arms, a precious burden. As for Gabriel Nolan, there was not a man in all the neighborhood who drank daily of a more precious wine of life than him. An angel had come into his house disguised as a sick, helpless, and miserable child, and filled all its dreary chambers with the sunshine of love.

Gabriel Nolan later took Clara to an orthopedic hospital. A doctor examined Clara and told Gabriel Nolan that there is a possibility of her using her legs again, but it will take quite a time with serious intensive care.

Mr. and Mrs. Gabriel Nolan accepted the doctor's report in good faith and made every possible effort they can.

Within nine months of living with Clara, Mrs. Gabriel became pregnant and gave birth to a son.

Mr. and Mrs. Gabriel Nolan loved Clara so much that they later officially adopt her and even changed her surname to Nolan.

Gabriel Nolan continued in his business but now works harder, knowing he would have more mouths to feed, but he now does it with great joy of a father and beloved husband.

The End.

The Stolen skeleton Arm

It happened when I was about eighteen or nineteen years old (began Dr. Simson). I was studying at the University, and being assisted by Solling a course mate on anatomy who is also an old friend. He was an amusing fellow, this Ivan. Full of jokes and playful ideas, and equally cheerful, whether he was working at the dissecting table or quarrelling with another guy in front of a jovial crowd, all he does is always comical.

He had but one fault—if I will call it so—and that was his exaggerated idea of punctuality. He grumbled if you were late two minutes; any longer delay would spoil the entire evening for him. He himself was never known to be late. At least, not during the entire years of my studying.

One Wednesday evening, our little circle of friends met, as usual, in my room at seven o'clock. I had made the customary preparations for the meeting, had borrowed three chairs—I have only one myself — and had persuaded Hans to take the breakfast dishes from the sofa and carry them downstairs. One by one, my friends arrived. The clock struck seven, and to our great astonishment, Solling had not yet appeared. One, two, even five minutes passed before we heard him run upstairs and knock at the door with his characteristic quick blows.

When he entered the room he looked so angry and at the same time so upset that I cried out: "What's the matter, Solling? You look as if you had been robbed."

"That's exactly what has happened," replied Solling angrily. "But it was no ordinary sneak thief," he added, hanging his overcoat behind the door.

"What have you lost?" asked my neighbor Nansen.

"Both arms from the new skeleton I've just recently received from the hospital," said Solling with an expression as if his last cent had been taken from him. "It's vandalism!"

We burst out into loud laughter at this remarkable answer, but Solling continued: "Can you imagine it? Both arms are gone, cut off at the shoulder joint; — and the strangest part of it is that the same thing has been done to my shabby old skeleton which stands in my bedroom. There wasn't an arm on either of them."

"That's too bad," I remarked. For we were just going to study the Anatomy of the arm tonight."

"Osteology," corrected Solling gravely. "Get out your skeleton, Simson. It isn't as good as mine, but it will do for this evening."

I went to the corner where my anatomical treasures were hidden behind a green curtain—"the Museum," was what Solling called it—but my astonishment was great when I found my skeleton in its accustomed place and wearing as usual my student's uniform, but without arms.

"What a devil!" cried Solling. "That was done by the same person who robbed me; the arms are taken off at the shoulder joint in exactly the same manner. You did it, Simson!"

I declared my innocence, very angry at the abuse of my fine skeleton, while Nansen cried: "Wait a minute, I'll go and get mine. There hasn't been a soul in my room since this morning, I can swear to that. I'll be back in a minute."

He hurried into his room, but returned in a few minutes, greatly depressed and somewhat ashamed. The skeleton was in its usual place, but the arms were gone, cut off at the shoulder in exactly the same manner as mine.

The affair, mysterious in itself, had now come to be a serious matter. We lost ourselves in suggestions and explanations, none of which seemed to throw any light on the subject. Finally, we sent a messenger to the other side of the house where, as I happened to know, was a new skeleton which the young student Ravn had recently received from the hospital.

Ravn had gone out and taken the key with him. The messenger whom we had sent to the rooms of the young students returned with the information that there been a fight over there and two people involved of had used the only skeleton they possessed to pummel each other with and that consequently only the thigh bones were left unbroken.

What were we to do? We couldn't understand the matter at all. Solling scolded and cursed and the company was about to break up when we heard someone coming noisily upstairs. The door was thrown open and a tall, thin figure appeared on the threshold—our good friend Niels Daae.

He was a strange guy, this Niels Daae, a rare type of human species found nowadays. He was no longer young, and by reason of a strange chain of circumstances, as he expressed it, he had been through nearly all the professions and could produce papers proving that he had been on the point of passing not one but three examinations.

He had begun with theology; but the story of the quarrel between Jacob and Esau had led him to take up the study of law. As a law student, he had come across an interesting poisoning case, which had proved to him that a study of medicine was extremely necessary for lawyers; and he had taken up the study of medicine with such energy that he had forgotten all his laws and was about to take his last examinations at the age of forty.

Niels Daae took the story of our missing bones very seriously. "Every pot has two handles," he began. "Every sausage two ends, every question two sides, except this one—this has three." (We A

Applauded for him to continue.) "When we look at it from the legal point of view, there can be no doubt that this will be classified into the category of ordinary theft. But from the fact that the thief took only the arms when he might have taken the entire skeleton, we must conclude that he is not in a responsible condition of mind, which therefore introduces a medical side to the affair. From a legal point of view, the thief must be convicted for robbery, or at least for the illegal appropriation of the property of others; but from the medical point of view, we must acquit him, because he is not sanely responsible for his acts. Here we have two professions quarreling with one another, and who shall say which is right? But now I will introduce the theological point of view and raise the entire affair up to a higher plane. Providence, in the material shape of a patron of mine in the country, whose children I have inoculated with the juice of wisdom, has sent me two fat geese and two first-class ducks. These animals are to be cooked and eaten this evening in Mathiesen's establishment, and I invite this honored company to join me there. Personally, I look upon the disappearance of these arms as an all- wise intervention of Providence, which sets its own inscrutable wisdom up against the wisdom which we would otherwise have heard from the lips of my venerable friend Solling."

Daae's confused speech was received with laughter and applause, and Solling's weak protests were lost in the general delight at the invitation. I have often noticed that such festivities made using whatever is available are usually the most enjoyable, and so it was for us that evening. Niels Daae treated us to his ducks and to his most amusing jokes, Solling sang his best songs, our jovial host Mathiesen told his humorous stories, and the merriment was in full swing when all of a sudden we heard cries in the street, and then a rush of confused noises broken by screams of pain.

"There's been an accident," cried Solling, running out to the door.

We all followed him and discovered that a car with failed breaks drove about madly, the driver making a desperate attempt to stop the car without running anybody over ran into an enormous tree nearby. His right arm had been broken near the shoulder. In the twinkling of an eye, the hall of festivities was transformed into an emergency hospital. Solling shook his head as he examined the injury, and ordered that we should wait for an ambulance to transport the patient to the city hospital. It was his belief that the arm would have to be amputated, cut off at the shoulder joint, just as had been the case with our skeleton. "What an odd coincidence, isn't it?" he remarked to me.

Our merry mood had vanished and we start to walk our way back, quiet and depressed, through the old avenues toward our home. For the first time since we occupied our venerable "barracks," as we called the dormitory, we its occupants returned home from an evening's bout just too early.

"Just eleven," exclaimed Solling. "It's too early to go to bed, and too late to go anywhere else. We'll go up to your room, little Simson, and see if we can have some kind of studies this evening. You have your colored plates and we'll try to get along with them. It's a nuisance that we should have lost those arms just this evening."

"There is a galore of bones now, so any doctor can have all the arms and legs he wants," grinned Hans, who came out of the doorway just in time to hear Solling's last word.

"What do you mean, Hans?" asked Solling in astonishment.

"It'll be easy enough to get them," said Hans. "They've torn down the planking around the Holy Trinity churchyard and dug up the earth to build a new wall. I saw it myself, as I came past the church. Lord, what a lot of bones they've dug out there! There're arms and legs and heads, many more than the Doctor could possibly need."

"This is to our own advantage," answered Solling. "They shut the gates at seven o'clock and it's after eleven already."

"Oh, yes, even if they shut them," grinned Hans again. "But there's another way to get in. If you go through the gate of the porcelain factory and over the courtyard, and through the mill in the fourth courtyard that leads out into Spring Street, there you will see where the planking is torn down, and you can get into the churchyard easily."

"Hans, you're a genius!" exclaimed Solling in delight. "Here, Simson, you know that factory inside and out? You're so friendly with that fellow Outzen who lives there. Run along to him and let him give you the key to the mill. It will be easy to find an arm that isn't too much decayed. Hurry along, now; the rest of us will wait for you upstairs."

To be quite honest, I must confess that I was not particularly eager to fulfill Solling's command. I was at an age to have still a sufficient amount of unpleasant emotions for death and the grave, and the mysterious occurrence of the stolen arms still ran through my mind. But I was still more afraid of Solling's pranks and of the laughter of my comrades which I am sure will be used to create seasonal pranks till I graduate from here, so I trotted off as carelessly as if I had been sent to buy a package of noodles.

It took me time to succeed in arousing the old janitor of the factory from his peaceful sleep. I told him that I had an important message for Outzen and hurried upstairs to the latter's room. Outzen was a strictly moral character; remembering this, I was prepared that he will surely refuse to give me the key which would let me into the fourth courtyard and from there into the cemetery. As I expected, Outzen took the matter very seriously. He closed the Hebrew Bible, which he had been studying as I entered, turned on his bedroom light, for he was reading with a reading light, and looked at me in astonishment as I made my request.

"Why, my dear Simson, it is a very sinful thing that you are about to do," he said gravely. "Take my advice and forget about it. You will get no key from me for any such cause. The peace of the grave is sacred. No man should disturb it."

"And how about the gravedigger? He puts the newly dead down beside the old corpses and lives as peacefully as anyone else."

"He is doing his duty," answered Outzen calmly. "But to disturb the peace of the grave from sheer adventure, with the fumes of the alcohol still in your head,—that is a different matter,—that will surely be punished!"

His words irritated me. It is not very flattering, particularly if one is not yet twenty, to be told that you are about to perform an adventurous deed, simply because you are drunk. Without any further reply to his protests, I rushed and took the key from its place on the wall and ran downstairs two steps at a time, vowing to myself that I would take home an arm. Who cares what the outcome will be? I would show Outzen, and Solling, and all the rest, what a brave guy I was.

My heart pounded as I stole through the long dark corridor, past the ruins of the old convent of St. Clara, into the so-called third courtyard. Here I took a flashlight from the hall that seems to belong to the janitor, switched it on. The light from it was dim; it was running out of battery. I crossed to the mill where the clay was prepared for the factory. The tall wheels and cylinders, with their straps and bolts, looked like weird creatures of the night in the dim light of my tallow flashlight. I felt my courage sinking even here, but I pulled myself together, opened the last door with my key and stepped out into the fourth courtyard. A moment later, I stood on the dividing line between the cemetery and the factory.

The entire length of the tall, blackened planking had been torn down. The pieces of it lay about, and the earth had been dug up to considerable depth, to make a foundation for a new wall between life and Death. The uncanny emptiness of the place was arresting to me. I halted involuntarily, as if to harden myself against it. It was a raw, cold, stormy evening. The clouds flew past the moon in jagged fragments, so that the churchyard, with its white crosses and stones, lay now in full light, now in dim shadow. Now and then a rush of wind rattled over the graves, roared through the leafless trees, bent the complaining bushes, and caught itself in the little eddy at the corner of the church, only to escape again over the roofs, turning the old weather vane with a sharp scream of the rusty iron.

I looked toward the left—there I saw several weird white shapes moving gently in the moonlight. "White sheets," I said to myself, "it's nothing but white sheets! This drying of linen in the churchyard ought to be stopped."

I turned in the opposite direction and saw a heap of bones scarce two paces distant from me. Holding my lower my flashlight, I approached them and stretched out my hand—there was a rattling in the heap; something warm and soft touched my fingers.

I started and shivered. Then I exclaimed: "The rats! Nothing but the rats in the churchyard! I must not get frightened. It will be so foolish—they would laugh and make fun of me. Where on earth is that arm? I can't find one that isn't broken!"

With trembling knees and in feverish haste, I examined one heap after another. The light in my flashlight start to blink as if the wind was blowing on it and suddenly went out. The foul smell of something decaying rose to my face, and I felt as if I were about to faint. It took all my energy to recover my control. I walked two or three steps ahead and saw at a little distance a coffin which had been still in good shape when taken out of the earth.

I approached it and saw that it was of old-fashioned shape, made of heavy oaken boards that were already rotting. On its cover was a metal plate with an illegible inscription. The old wood was so brittle that it would have been very easy for me to open the coffin with any sort of tool. I looked about me and saw a hatchet and a couple of spades lying near the fence. I took one of the latter, put its flat end between the boards—the old coffin fell apart with a dull crackling protest.

I turned my head aside, put my hand in through the opening, felt about, and, taking a firm hold on one arm of the skeleton, I loosened it from the body with a quick jerk. The movement loosened the head as well, and it rolled out through the opening right to my very feet. I took up the skull to lay it in the coffin again—and then I saw a greenish phosphorescent glimmer in its empty eye sockets, a glimmer which came and went. Mad terror shook me at the sight. I looked up at the houses in the distance, then back again to the skull; the empty sockets shone more brightly than before. I felt that I must have some natural explanation for this appearance or I would go mad. I took up the head again—and never in my life have I had so overpowering an impression of the might of death and decay than in this moment. Countless disgusting moist insects poured out of every opening of the skull, and a couple of shining, wormlike centipedes—Geophilus, the scientists call them—crawled about in the eye sockets. I threw the skull back into the coffin, sprang over the heaps of bones without even taking time to pick up my flashlight, and ran like a hunted thing through the dark mill, over the factory courtyards, until I reached the outer gate. There I washed the arm at the fountain and smoothed my disarranged clothing. I hid my booty under my overcoat, nodded to the sleepy old janitor as he opened the door to me, and a few moments later I entered my own room with an expression which I had attempted to make quite calm and careless.

"What on earth is the matter with you, Simson?" cried Solling as he saw me. "Have you seen a ghost? Or is the alcohol wearing off already? We thought you'd never come; why, it's nearly twelve o'clock!"

Without a word, I drew back my overcoat and laid my booty on the table.

"O my God," exclaimed Solling in anatomical enthusiasm, "where did you find that superb arm? Simson knows what needed, all right. It's a girl's arm; isn't it beautiful? Just look at the hand—how fine and delicate it is! Must have worn a size 7 glove. This is a pretty hand to caress and kiss!"

The arm passed from one to the other in general admirations. Every word that was said increased my disgust for myself and for what I had done. It was a woman's arm, then—what sort of woman might she have been? Young and beautiful, possibly—her brothers' pride, her parents' joy. She had faded away in her youth, cared for by loving hands and tender thoughts. She had fallen asleep gently, and those who loved her had desired to give her in death the peace she had enjoyed throughout her lifetime. For they had made her coffin of thick, heavy oaken boards. And this hand, loved and missed by so many—it lay there now on an anatomical table, encircled by clouds of tobacco smoke, stared at by curious glances, and made the object of coarse jokes. O God! How terrible it was!

"I must have that arm," exclaimed Solling, when the first burst of admiration had passed. "When I bleach it and touch it up with varnish, it wild be a superb specimen. I'll take it home with me."

"No," I exclaimed, "I can't permit it. It was wrong of me to bring it away from the churchyard. I'm going right back to put the arm in its place once we are through."

"Well, will you listen to that?" cried Solling, amid the hearty laughter of the others. "Simson's so lyric, he certainly must be drunk. I must have that arm at any cost."

"Not much," cut in Niels Daae; "you have no right to it. It was buried in the earth and dug out again; it belongs to nobody, and all the rest of us have just as much right to it as you have."

"Yes, everyone of us has some share in it," said someone else.

"But what are you going to do about it?" remarked Solling. "It would be vandalism to break up that arm. What God has joined together, let no man put asunder," he concluded with pathos.

"Let's auction it off," exclaimed Daae. "I will be the auctioneer, and this key to the graveyard will serve me as a hammer."

The laughter broke out anew as Daae took his place solemnly at the head of the table and began to whine out the following announcement: "I hereby notify all present that on the 25th of November, at twelve o'clock at midnight, in corridor No. 5 of the student barracks, a lady's arm in excellent condition, with all its appurtenances of wrist bones, joints, and fingertips, is to be offered at public auction. The buyer can have possession of his purchase immediately after the auction, and a credit of six weeks will be given to any reliable customer. I bid a cent."

"One dollar," cried Solling mockingly.

"Two," cried somebody else.

"Four," exclaimed Solling. “It's worth it. Why don't you join in,” Simson? You look as if you were sitting in a hornet's nest."

I bid one dollar more, and Solling added a dollar more. There were no more bids. The hammer fell, and the arm belonged to Solling.

"Here, take this," he said, handing me a dollar bill; "it's part of your commission as a grave robber. You shall have the rest later, unless you prefer that I should turn it over to the drinking fund." With these words, Solling wrapped the arm in a newspaper, and the jolly crowd ran noisily down the stairs and through the streets, until their singing and laughter were lost in the distance.

I stood alone, still bewildered, staring at the piece of money in my hand. My thoughts were far too much agitated that I should hope to sleep. I turned off the light and switch on my reading lamp and took out one of my books to try to study myself into a quieter mood. But without success.

Suddenly, I heard a sound like that of a swinging pendulum. I raised my head and listened attentively. There was no clock either in my room or in the neighboring ones—but I could still hear the sound. At the same moment, my reading lamp began to flicker. I was about to rise and switch on the room lights again when my eyes fell upon the door, and I saw the graveyard key, which I had hung there, moving slowly back and forth with a rhythmic swing. Just as its motion seemed about to die away, it would receive a gentle push as from an unseen hand, and would swing back and forth more than ever. I stood there with an open mouth and staring eyes. Ice-cold chills ran down my back, and drops of perspiration stood out on my forehead. Finally, I could endure it no longer. I sprang to the door, seized the key with both hands and put it on my desk under a pile of heavy books. Then I breathed a sigh of relief.

My reading lamp went off, and I discovered that the electricity in the entire neighborhood was cut off. With feverish haste, I threw my clothes off, and sprang into bed as if to smother my fears.

But once alone in the darkness, the fears grew worse than ever. They grew into dreams and visions. It seemed to me as if I were out in the graveyard again, and heard the screaming of the rusty weather vane as the wind turned it. Then I was in the old mill again; the wheels were turning and stretching out ghostly hands to draw me into the yawning maw of the machine. Then again, I found myself in a long, low, pitch-black corridor, followed by Something I could not see—Something that drove me to the mouth of a bottomless abyss. I would start up out of my half sleep, listen and look about me, then fall back again into an uneasy sleep.

Suddenly something fell from the ceiling onto the bed, and "buzz — buzz—buzz" sounded in my head. It was a huge fly which had been sleeping in a corner of my room. It flew about in great circles, now around the bed, now in all four corners of the chamber—"buzz—buzz, buzz". It was unendurable! At last I heard it creep into a bag of sugar which had been left on the windowsill. I sprang up and closed the bag tight. The fly buzzed worse than ever, but I went back to bed and attempted to sleep again, feeling that I had conquered the enemy.

I began to count: I counted slowly to one hundred, two hundred, finally up to one thousand, and then at last I experienced that pleasant weakness, which is the forerunner of true sleep. I seemed to be in a beautiful garden, bright with many flowers and fragrance with all the perfumes of spring. At my side walked a beautiful young girl. I seemed to know her well, and yet it was not possible for me to remember her name, or even to know how we came to be wandering there together. As we strolled through the paths, she stopped to pick a flower or to admire a brilliant butterfly swaying in the air. Suddenly, a cold wind blew through the garden. The young girl trembled and her cheeks grew pale. "I am cold," she said to me, "can't you see? It is Death who is approaching us."

I would have answered, but at that instance another stronger and still icier gust roared through the garden. The leaves turned pale on the trees, the flowerets bent their heads, and the bees and butterflies fell lifeless to the earth. "That is Death," whispered my companion, trembling.

A third icy gust blew the last leaves from the bushes. White crosses and gravestones appeared between the bare twigs—and I was in the churchyard again and heard the screaming of the rusty weather vane. Beside me stood a heavy brass-bound coffin with a metal plate on the cover. I bent down to read the inscription; the cover rolled off suddenly, and from out the coffin rose the young girl who had been with me in the garden. I stretched out my arms to clasp her to my breast—then, oh horror! I saw the greenish-gleaming, empty eye sockets of the skull. I felt bony arms around me, dragging me back into the coffin. I screamed aloud for help and woke up.

My room seemed unusually lighted; but I remembered that it was a moonlight night and thought no more of it. I tried to explain the visions of my dream with various natural noises about me. The imprisoned fly buzzed as loudly as a whole swarm of bees; one half of my window had blown open, and the cold night air rushed in gusts into my room.

I sprang up to close the window, and then I saw that the strong white light that filled my room did not come from the moon, but seemed to shine out from the church opposite. I heard the chiming of the bells, soft at first, as if in the far distance, then stronger and stronger until, mingled with the rolling notes of the Church organ, a mighty rush of sound struck against my windows. I stared out into the street and could scarcely believe my eyes. The houses in the marketplace just beyond were all little one-story buildings with bow windows and wooden wave troughs ending in carved dragon heads. Most of them had balconies of carved woodwork, and high stone stoops with gleaming brass rails.

But it was the church most of all that aroused my astonishment. Its position was completely changed. Its front turned toward our house where usually the side had stood. The church was brilliantly lighted, and now I perceived that it was this light which filled my room. I stood speechless amid the chiming of the bells and the roaring of the organ, and I saw a long wedding procession moving slowly up the center aisle of the church toward the altar. The light was so brilliant that I could distinguish each one of the figures. They were all in strange old-time costumes; the ladies in brocades and satins with strings of pearls in their powdered hair, the gentlemen in uniform with knee breeches, swords, and cocked hats held under their arms. But it was the bride who drew my attention most strongly. She was clothed in white satin, and a faded myrtle wreath was twisted through the powdered locks beneath her sweeping veil. The bridegroom at her side wore a red uniform and many decorations. Slowly they approached the altar, where an old man in black vestments and a heavy white wig was awaiting them. They stood before him, and I could see that he was reading the ritual from a gold-lettered book.

One of the train stepped forward and unbuckled the bridegroom's sword, that his right hand might be free to take that of the bride. She seemed about to raise her own hand to his when she suddenly sank, fainting at his feet. The guests hurried toward the altar; the lights went out, the music stopped, and the figures floated together like pale white mists.

But outside in the square it was still brighter than before, and I suddenly saw the side portal of the church burst open and the wedding procession move out across the marketplace.

I turned as if to flee, but could not move a muscle. Quietly, as if turned to stone, I stood and watched the ghostly figures that came nearer and nearer. The clergyman led the train, and then came the bridegroom and the bride, and as the latter raised her eyes to me I saw that it was the young girl of the garden. Her eyes were so full of pain, so full of a sad plea that I could scarce endure them; but how shall I explain the feeling that shot through me as I suddenly discovered that the right sleeve of her white satin gown hung empty at her side? The train disappeared, and the tone of the church bells changed to a strange, dry, creaking sound, and the gate below me complained as it turned on its rusty hinges. I faced toward my own door. I knew that it was shut and locked, but I knew that the ghostly procession was coming to call me to account, and I felt that no walls could keep them out. My door flew open. There was a rustling as of silken gowns, but the figures seemed to float in the changing forms of swaying white mists. Closer and closer they gathered around me, robbing me of breath, robbing me of the power to move. There was a silence as of the grave—and then I saw before me the old priest with his gold-lettered book. He raised his hand and spoke with a soft, deep voice: "The grave is sacred! Let no one dare to disturb the peace of the dead."

"The grave is sacred!" an echo rolled through the room as the swaying figures moved like reeds in the wind.

"What do you want? What do you demand?" I gasped in the grip of a deathly fear.

"Give back to the grave that which belongs to it," said the deep voice again.

"Give back to the grave that which belongs to it," repeated the echo as the swaying forms pressed closer to me.

"But it's impossible—I can't—I have sold it; sold it at auction!" I screamed in despair. "It was buried and found on the earth—and sold for five dollars eight cents—"

A hideous scream came from the ghostly ranks. They threw themselves upon me as the white fog rolls in from the sea. They pressed upon me until I could no longer breathe. Beside myself, I threw open the window and attempted to spring out, screaming aloud: "Help! help! Murder! they are murdering me!"

The sound of my own voice awoke me. I found myself in my nightclothes on the windowsill, one leg already out of the window and both hands clutching at the center post. On the street below me stood the night watchman, staring up at me in astonishment, while faint white clouds of mist rolled out of my window like smoke. All around outside lay the November fog, gray and moist, and as the fresh air of the early dawn blew cool on my face, I felt my senses returning to me. I looked down at the night watchman—God bless him! He was a big, strong, comfortably fat fellow made of real flesh and blood, and no ghost shape of the night. I looked at the round tower of the church—how massive and venerable it stood there, gray in the gray of the morning mists. I looked over at the marketplace. There was a light in the baker's shop and a farmer stood before it with his bicycle. Back in my own room, everything was in its usual place. Even the little paper bag with the sugar lay there on the windowsill, and the imprisoned fly buzzed louder than ever. I knew that I was really awake and that the day was coming. I sprang back hastily from the window and was about to jump into bed when my foot touched something hard and sharp.

I stooped to see what it was, felt about on the floor in the half light, and touched a long, dry, skeleton arm which held a tiny roll of paper in its bony fingers. I felt about again, and found still another arm, also holding a roll of paper. Then I began to think that I was going insane. What I had seen thus far was only an unusually vivid dream—a vision of my heated imagination. But I knew that I was awake now, and yet here lay two-no, three (for there was still another arm)—hard, undeniable, material proofs that what I had thought was hallucination, might have been reality. Trembling at the thought that madness was threatening me, I tore open the first roll of paper. On it was written the name: "Solling." I caught at the second and opened it. There stood the word: "Nansen." I had just strength enough left to catch the third paper and open it—there was my own name: "Simson."

Then I sank, fainting to the floor.

When I came to myself again, Niels Daae stood beside me with an empty water bottle, the contents of which were dripping off my person and off the sofa upon which I was lying. "Here, drink this," he said in a soothing tone. "It will make you feel better."

I looked about me wildly, as I sipped at the glass of brandy which put new life into me once more. "What has happened?" I asked weakly.

"Oh, nothing of importance," answered Niels. "You were just about to be suffocated by the smoke from this burning home appliance," pointing at the heater in the room "the wind must have obstructed something in the power source and the electric power went out but came back after some minutes with abnormal heavy voltage and that triggered the fire from the appliance. If you had not opened the window, you would have already been too far along the path to Paradise to be called back by a glass of brandy. Take another."

"How did you get up here?" I asked, sitting upright on the sofa.

"Through the door in the usual simple manner," answered Niels Daae. "I was on watch last night in the hospital; but Mathiesen's alcohol is heavy and my watching was more like sleeping, so I thought it better to come away in the early morning. As I passed your barracks here, I saw you sitting in the window in your nightshirt and calling down to the night watchman that someone was murdering you. I managed to wake up Jansen down below you and got into the house through his window. Do you usually sleep walk?"

"But where did the arms come from?" I asked, still half bewildered.

"Oh, those god dam arms," cried Niels. "Just see if you can stand up all right now. Oh, those arms there? Why, those are the arms I cut off your skeletons. Clever idea, wasn't it? You know how grumpy Solling gets if anything interferes with his lecturing. You see, I'd had the geese sent me, and I wanted you all to come with me to Mathiesen's place. I knew you were going to read the osteology of the arm, so I went up into Solling's room, opened it with his own keys and took the arms from his skeleton. I did the same here while you were downstairs in the reading room. Have you been stupid enough to take them down off their frames and take away their tickets? I had marked them so carefully that each man should get his own again."

I dressed hastily and went out with Niels into the fresh, cool morning air. A few minutes later we separated, and I turned toward the street where Solling lived. Without heeding the protest of his old landlady, I entered the room where he was still fast asleep. The arm, still wrapped in newspaper, lay on his desk. I took it up, put the mark piece in its place and hastened with all speed to the churchyard.

How different it looked in the early dawn! The fog had risen and shining frost pearls hung in the bare twigs of the tall trees where the sparrows were already twittering their morning song. There was no one to be seen. The churchyard lay quiet and peaceful. I stepped over the heaps of bones to where the heavy oaken coffin lay under a tree. Cautiously I pushed the arm back into its interior, and hammered the rusty nails into their places again, just as the first rays of the pale November sun touched a gleam of light from the metal plate on the cover.—Then the weight was lifted from my soul.

The End

Enigmatical Manuscript

Two gentlemen sat chatting together one evening.

Their daily business was to occupy themselves with literature. At the present moment they were engaged in drinking whisky,—an activity both agreeable and useful to both of them,—they were also chatting about books, movies, women and many other things. Finally, they came around to that inexhaustible subject for conversation, the unexplainable mysterious occurrences in life, the hidden things, the Unknown, Mr. X, now. Raising his glass, he looked at himself meditatively in a mirror opposite, and, in an excellent imitation of the character of his favorite actor, he quoted:

"There are more things in heaven and earth than are dreamt of in philosophy and unexplained by science with all scientific experiments. It is clear that we humans are still scratching the surface of what life has to offer. Each empire thinks they have to arrive at 'It', the center, only for another to overtake them, outdated and obsolete the other in new and unimaginable discoveries and explanations. "

Mr. Y. arranged a fresh glass for himself and answered,

"I believe it. I believe also that it is given but to a few chosen ones to see these things. I know I am never among those lucky ones. Or fortunately for me, perhaps. For,—at least so it appears to me, — these chosen ones on closer investigation appear to be individuals of unusual mental capabilities or if not so then people of abnormal brain condition. As far as I am concerned personally, I know of nothing more strange than the usual logical and natural sequence of events on our globe. I confess things do sometimes happen outside of this orderly sequence; but for the think tanks and thoughtful person, the Strange, the apparently Inexplicable, usually turns out to be a coincidence, a sum of Chance, that Chance we will never be quite clever enough to fully take into our calculations.

"As an instance I would like to tell you the story of what happened several years back to a friend of mine, a young French writer. He had a good and sincere behavior. The event of which I am about to tell you threw him into what was almost a delirium, which came near to robbing him of his intelligence, and therefore came near to robbing his beloved readers of a few excellent books.

"This was the way it happened:

"It was about ten years back, and I was spending the spring and summer in Paris. I had a room with the family of a concierge on the left bank, Rue de Vaugirard, near the Luxembourg Gardens.

"A few steps from my modest domicile lived my friend Lucien F. We had become acquainted through a chain of circumstances which have no link to this story, but those circumstances had made our friendship firm, we had a lot of good times together and he also assisted me to have a better understanding of how life is in Paris. This friendship also enabled me to enjoy better and cheaper whisky than one can usually get within the city.'

"Lucien F. had already published several books which had aroused attention through the maverick of its unusual niche, and their gratifying success had made it possible for him to be established financially, with a comfortably furnished bachelor apartment on the corner of the Rue de Vaugirard and the rue de Conde.

"The apartment had a corridor and three rooms; a dining room, a bedroom and a charming study with an inclosed balcony, the three windows of which,—a large one in the center and two smaller ones at the side,—sent a flood of light in over the great writing table which filled nearly the entire balcony. Inside the room, near the balcony, stood a divan couch covered with an animal fur. Upon this divan couch, I spent many of my hours in Paris, occupied in the smoking of my friend's excellent cigars, and the sampling of his superlatively good whisky. It feels like lying down and staring up at the tops of the trees in Luxembourg Gardens, while Lucien worked at his desk. For, unlike most writers, he could work best when he was not alone.

"If I remained away several days, he would invariably ring my bell early in the morning, and drag me out of bed with the remark: 'The whisky is ready. I can't write if you are not there.'

"In one of those days of which I am about to tell you, he was engaged in writing a fantastic novelette with the title, 'The Force of the Wind,' a work which captivated him so much and he was heavily engrossed in it, but he would interrupt himself unwillingly at intervals to finish and furnish a column for a well- known newspaper that numbered him among their staffs. His books were also printed by the same newspaper house.

"Often, as I lay in my favorite position on the divan, the bell would ring and we would be visited by the printer's boy Adolphe, a little fellow who wears blue shirt, the genuine type of Paris street boy. Adolphe has a broken nose, a pair of crafty eyes, and had his fists always full of manuscripts which he treated with a carelessness that would have driven a literary novice to despair. This paper company that hired Adolphe for a part-time work did so because they have had issues where their client's submitted damaged soft copies of their manuscript and also where the soft copies were tapped, hacked altered or stolen from the computer network before it could get to them so they decide that the manuscript should be accepted in hard copies (paper form) and not in software form a measure to prevent a reoccurrence of previous incidence. The long rolls of paper would hang out of Adolphe's backpack as if ready to fall apart at his next movement. And the disrespectful manner in which he crammed my friend Lucien's essay into his backpack would have certainly called forth remarks from a journalist of more self- conceit.

"But his eyes were so full of sly cunning, and there was this in-depth understanding of street life in Paris about the heavily built, little fourteen-year-old chap, that we would often keep him longer with us, and treat him to a bottle of soft drink in other to hear his opinion of the writers whose work he handled. He was an amusing cross between a tricky little modern Paris ‘gamin’ and a home bred child, and he hit off the characteristics of the various writers with as keen a touch of actuality as he could put into his stories of how many centimes he had won that morning at 'craps' from his friend Pierre. Pierre was another employee of the printing house, Adolphe's comrade in his study of the mysteries of Paris streets, but now his rival. They were both in love with the same girl; the fifteen-year-old daughter of the keeper of 'La Prunelle' Cafe, and her favor was often the prize of the morning's game.

"Now and then, this rivalry between the two young boys would turn into a hand-to-hand fight. I myself was witness to such a fight one day, in front of 'La Prunelle.' The rivals punched each other terribly while the manuscripts flew about over the pavement, and Virginie, in her short skirts, stood at the door of the cafe and drown herself with laughter until she seemed about to shake to pieces.

"Pierre was stronger than his opponent, and Adolphe came off with a bloody nose. He gathered up his manuscripts in stern silence and left the battlefield staring at the still laughing Virginie with an expression of deep anger on his wounded face.

"The following day, when I teased him a little because of his defeat, he smiled a sly smile and remarked:

"'Yes, but I won a lot of francs from him, the big stupid animal. And so it was I, after all, who took Virginie out that evening. We went to the Cafe, Neant, where I let them put me in the coffin and pretend to be decaying, to amuse her. She found it so funny.'

"One morning Lucien had come for me as usual, dragged me to the divan, and commenced his work at his writing table. He was just putting the last words to his novel, and the table was entirely covered with the scattered leaves, closely written. I could just see his neck as he sat there, a thin-sinewed, expressive neck. He bent over his work, blind and deaf to everything around him. I lay there and gazed out at the top of the trees in the park up into the blue summer sky. The window on the left side of the desk stood wide open, for it was a warm and sultry day. I sipped my drink slowly. The air was heavy, and thunder threatened in the distance. After a little while, the clouds gathered together, heavy, low-hanging, copper- hued, real thunderclouds, and the trees in the park rustled softly. The air was stifling, and lay heavy as lead on my breast.

"'Lucien!'

"Lucien did not hear or see anything. His pen flew over the paper.

"I fell hack lazily on my divan.

"Then, suddenly, there was a mighty tumult. A powerful gust of wind swept through the street, bending the trees in the gardens quite out of my horizon. With a crash the right-hand window in the balcony flew wide open, and like a cyclone, the wind swept through, clearing the table in an instant of all the loose sheets of paper that had lain scattered about it.

"'What on earth! Why don't you shut the window!' I cried, springing up from the sofa.

"'Spare your energy, it's too late,' said Lucien with a gentle mockery in his soft voice. 'Look there!'—he pointed out into the street, where his sheets of paper went swirling about in the heavy air like white doves.

"A second later came the rain, a veritable cloud-burst. We shut the windows and gave ourselves up to sad and painful thoughts about the lost manuscript, the recovery of which now seemed utterly hopeless.

"'That's thousands of francs that the wind has robbed me of,' sighed Lucien. 'Well, am okay, that doesn't matter so much. But do you know anything more tiresome than to work on the same subject a second time? I can't think of doing it. It would surely make me sick to try it.'

"We were in a sad mood that morning. When we went out to breakfast at about two o'clock, we looked about for some traces of the lost manuscript.

"There was nothing to be seen. It had vanished completely, whirled off to all four corners of the earth probably, this manuscript from which Lucien had expected so much. Truly it was 'The Force of the Wind.'

. . . . .

"Now comes the strange part of the story. One morning, two weeks later, Lucien stood in the door of my little room, pale as a ghost. He had a bundle of printer's proofs in his hand and held them out to me without a word.

"I looked at it and read:

"'"The Force of the Wind," by Lucien F.'

"It was a good bundle of proofs, the entire first proofs of Lucien's novel, the novel of the manuscript of which we had seen blown out of the balcony window and whirled away by the winds.

"'My dear man,' I exclaimed, as I handed him back the proofs. 'You have been industrious indeed, to write your entire novel over again in so short a time—and to have proofs already—'

"Lucien did not answer. He stood silent, staring at me with a weird look in his otherwise so sensible eyes. After a moment, he stammered,

"'I did not write the novel over again. I have not touched a pen since the day the manuscript blew out of the window.'

"'Are you a sleep-walker, Lucien?'

"'Why do you ask?'

"'Why I asked? Because that would be the only natural explanation. They say we can do many great things in sleep, of which we don't even know how to do when we wake. I've heard queer stories of that. Men who have committed murders in their sleep. It happens quite often that sleep-walkers write letters in a handwriting they do not recognize when awake.'

"'I have never been a sleep-walker,' answered Lucien.

"'Oh, you never can tell,' I remarked. 'Would you rather explain it as magic? Or was the work of fairies? Or do you believe in ghosts? Your stimulus has fascinated you, you mystic!' And I laughed and trilled a line from

'The Mascot,' which we had seen the evening before at the Lyric.

"But my attempt to distract his mood did not seem to strike an answering note in Lucien. He turned from me in silence, and with an offended expression took his cap and his proofs, and—humorist and skeptic as he was ordinarily, he parted from me with the words uttered in a theatrical tone:

"' There are more things in heaven and earth than are dreamt of in philosophy and unexplained by science with all scientific experiments.'

"He turned on his heel and left the room.

"To be sincere, I was affected by the brief scene. I was mystified. I could not for an instant doubt Lucien's honesty.—he was so shocked, so frightened — so touching down to the depth of his soul. Of course, the only explanation that I could see was that he had written his novel in a sleep-walking state.

"For certainly no printer could set up type from a manuscript that did not exist,—to say nothing of printing it and sending out proofs.

"Several days passed, but Lucien did not come near me. I went to his place once or twice, but the door was locked. What has happened to him? Or had this strange and inexplicable occurrence robbed him of his sanity and robbed me of his friendship and his excellent drink?

"After three useless attempts to find him at home, and after calling this mobile phone which he did not answer, I gave up visiting Lucien without any further attempt to understand his enigmatical behavior. Not after making a report at the police station. They later told me that they were able to reach him, that he was okay. A short time after, I left for my home without having seen or heard anything more of him.

. . . . .

"Months passed. I remained at home, and one evening, during the course of a nice party, the conversation came around to the subject of mysticism and supernatural occurrences. I dished up my story of the enigmatical manuscript. The Unknown, the supernatural and the Occult, was the trending thing at the moment, and my story was received with great applause and my title quotation That is 'more things in heaven and earth...' was wildly adopted by may. I came to think so much of it myself that I wrote about it and sent it to Professor Flammarion, who was just then making a study of the Unknown, which he adopted in his later book 'The Unknown.'

"Occupying myself with the story brought my mind around again to memories of Lucien. One day, I saw a notice in Le Figaro that his book, 'The Force of the

Wind,' had appeared in a second large edition, and had aroused much attention, particularly in spiritualistic circles. I seemed to see him again before me, with the facial expression he had the last time I saw him. The vision of this face rose up before me whenever I drink the same sort of drink that I had drunk so often with him, and I started longing to see or hear from my lost friend. I sat down one evening when in a sentimental mood, and typed a long text message to him, asking him to tell me something of himself and to send me a copy of his book. He did not respond to the message.

"But a week later, I received the little book and the following letter, which I have here in my pocket. It is somewhat crumpled, for I have read it several times. But even at that. I will read it to you now, if you will pardon my awkward translating of the French original.

"Here it is:

"DEAR FRIEND:

"Many thanks for your message. I am sorry I did not respond or call you immediately. For my friend, this book has turned me into a celebrity with one activity to another. A never-ending process. Here is the book. I have to thank you also that you did not lay my behavior of your last days in Paris up against me. It must have seemed strange to you. I will try to explain it.

"I have been nervous since childhood. The fact that most of my books have treated of fantastic subjects,—somewhat in the manner of Edgar Allan Poe—has made me more susceptible for all that world which lies beyond and about the world of every-day life. I have sought after,—and yet feared—the mystical; cool and lucid as I can be at times, I have always had an inclination for the enigmatical, the Unknown.

"But the first thing that ever happened in my life that I could not explain or understand was the affair of the manuscript. You remember the day I stood in your room? I must have looked like a masterpiece painting of misery. The affair had played more havoc with my nerves than you can very well understand. Your mockery hurt me, and yet under all I felt ashamed of my own thoughts concerning this foolish occurrence. I could not explain the phenomenon, and I shivered at the things that it suggested to me. For several weeks, I was in this condition. I could not bear to see you or anyone else, and I was impolite enough even to leave your calls unanswered.

"The book appeared and made a hit, since that sort of thing was the center of interest just then. But almost a month passed before I could arouse myself from that condition of fear and—I had almost said, softening of the brain—which prevented my enjoyment of my success.

"Then the explanation came. Thanks to this occurrence, I know now that I shall never again be in danger of being 'haunted.'

"And I know now that Chance can bring about stranger happenings than can any wish for visitations from the spirit world. Here you have the story of this 'mystic' occurrence, which came near endangering my sanity, and which turns out to be a chance combination of a gust of wind, a sudden downpour of rain, and the strange elements in the character of our little friend Adolphe the printer's boy.

"You remember that funny little guy with the crafty eye, his talent for gambling, and his admiration for the girl of 'La Prunelle'? An unusual little mixture for this child who has himself alone to look to for livelihood and care, the typical specie of the Paris streets wise, the modified gamin from 'Les Miserables.'

"About a month after the appearance of my book I lay on the divan one day,—your favorite place, you remember?—and lost myself in idle reasonings on the same old subject that never left my mind day or night, when the bell rang and Adolphe appeared, to pick up the essay on 'Le Boulevarde.' There was an unusually nervous gleam in his eyes that day. I gave him a drink and tried to find out what his trouble was. I did find it out, and I found out a good deal more besides.

"Thanks to his good fortune as a gambler, Virginie came to look upon him with favor. Pierre was quite out of the race and Adolphe's affection was reciprocated as much as his heart could desire. But with his good fortune in love came all the suffering, all the torture, the suspicions that tear the hearts of us men when we set our hopes upon a woman's truth. Young as he was, he went through them all, and now he was torturing himself with the thought that she did not really love him and was only pretending, while she gave her heart to another. Perhaps he was right—why not?

"I talked to Adolphe as man to man and managed to bring back a gleam of his usual jollity and sly humor. He took another glass of drink and blurted,

"'M. Lucien—I did something—'

"'Did what?' I asked.

"'Something I should have told you long ago—it was wrong, and you've always been so nice to me—'

"You remember the day, two months ago, when we had such a sudden wind and rain storm, a regular cloud-burst? I was down here in this neighborhood fetching manuscripts from M. Labouchere and M. Laroy. I was supposed to come up here for your copies, too. But then—you'll understand, after all I've been telling you,—I came around past 'La Prunelle' and Virginie stood in the doorway, and she'd promised to go out with me that evening. So I ran up to speak to her. And then when I went on again, I saw a sheet with your writing lying in the street. You know I know all the news papers contributor's handwriting, whose copy I fetch. Then I was frightened. I thought to myself, 'O my God,' I thought, 'here I've lost M. Lucien's manuscript.' I couldn't remember calling for it, but I thought I must have done so before I got M. Laroy's. Virginie is the only person I think about this days. I took up the sheet and saw three others a little further on. And I saw a lot more shining just behind the railing of the Luxembourg Garden. You know how hard it rained. The water held the paper down, so the wind couldn't carry it any further. I ran into the Garden and picked up all the sheets, thirty-two of them. All of them, except the first four I found in the street, had blown in behind the railing. And I can tell you I was precious, glad that I had them all together. I ran back to the office, told them I had dropped the manuscript in the street, but asked them not to say anything to you about it. But the sheets were all there,—you always number them so clearly, and 'handsome August,' the proofreader promised he wouldn't tell on me. I knew if the foreman heard of it, he'd fire me immediately, for he had a grudge against me. So nobody knew anything about it. But I thought I ought to tell you, 'cause you've been so nice to me. Maybe you'll understand how one gets crazy at times, when a girl like Virginie tells you she likes you better than Pierre, and yet you think she might deceive you for his sake—that big, stupid animal — But now I'll be going. Much obliged for your kindness, M. Lucien, and for the drink—' And he left me.

"There you have the explanation, the very simple and natural explanation of the phenomenon that almost drove me crazy.

"The entire 'supernatural' occurrence was caused by a careless boy's love affairs, by a gust of southwest wind, by a sudden heavy rain, and by the chance that I had used a special ink pen, the kind that water cannot blur. All these simple natural things made me act so foolishly toward a good friend, the sort of friend I have always known you to be. Let me hear from you and tell me what you people up North think of my book. I give you my word that the 'Unknown Powers' shall never again make me foolish enough to risk losing your friendship!

"Yours

"LUCIEN."

"So this is my story. Yes, 'there are more things in heaven and earth—' But the workings of Chance are the strangest of all. And this whisky is really very good. Here's to you."

The End

The Mysterious Room

For many years there stood in a side street in Kiel, a modest old stone house which had a threatening, almost sinister appearance, with its old-fashioned balcony and it is overhanging upper stories. For the last twenty years, the house had been occupied by a widow who is greatly respected, Madame Wolff, as she is called inherited from the house. She lived there quietly with her one and only daughter, in somewhat impoverished circumstances.

What augmented the mysterious notoriety of the house's sinister appearance was the fact that one of its rooms, a corner room on the main floor, had not been opened for generations. The door was firmly fastened and sealed with plaster, as well as the window looking out upon the street. Above the door was an old inscription, dated 1603, which threatened sudden death and eternal damnation to any human being who dared to open the door or erase the inscription. Neither door nor window had been opened in the two hundred years that had passed since the inscription was put up. But for a generation back or more, the partition wall and the sealed door had been covered with wallpaper, and the inscription had been almost forgotten.

The room adjoining the sealed chamber was a large hall, utilized only for rare important events. Such an occasion arose with the wedding of the only daughter of the house. For that evening, the great hall, as it was called, was brilliantly decorated and illuminated for a ball. The building had deep cellars and the old floors were elastic. Madame Wolff tried her best to avoid using the great hall at all, for the foolish old legend of the sealed chamber aroused a certain superstitious dread in her heart, and she rarely, if ever, entered the hall herself. But her pretty young daughter, Miss Elizabeth, was passionately fond of dancing, and her mother had promised that she would have a ball on her wedding day. Her betrothed, Winther a Secretary in the public service, was also a superb dancer, and the two young people persuaded and pester the mother's phobia against the hall and laughed at her fear of the sealed room. They thought it would be wiser to ignore the stupid legend altogether, and thus to force the world to forget it. In spite of the secret fear and uneasiness, Madame Wolff surrendered to their arguments. And for the first time in many years, the merry strains of dance music were heard in the great hall that lay next to the mysterious sealed chamber.

The bridal couple, as well as the wedding guests, were in their happiest mood, and the ball was an undoubted success. The dancing was interrupted for an hour while a meal was served in an adjoining room. After the repast, the guests returned to the hall, and it was several hours more before the last dance was called. The season was early autumn, and the weather was still balmy. The windows had been opened to freshen the air. But the walls retained their dampness and suddenly the dancers noticed that the old wall paper which covered the partition wall between the hall and the sealed chamber had been loosened through the jarring of the building, and had fallen away from the sealed door exposing the mysterious inscription.

The story of the sealed chamber was almost forgotten by most of those present, forgotten with its many other old legends heard in childhood. The sight of the inscription suddenly aroused great interest, and there was a general curiosity to know what the mysterious closed room might hide. speculations flew from mouth to mouth. Some insisted that the closed door must hide the traces of an extremely ugly murder, or some other equally terrible crime. Others suggested that perhaps the room had been used as a hiding place for clothes and other articles belonging to some person who had died of an epidemic, and that the room had been sealed for fear of spreading the disease. Still others thought that in the sealed chamber there might be found a secret entrance from the cellars, which had made the room available as a hiding place for robbers or smugglers. The guests had quite forgotten their dancing in the interest, awakened by the sight of the mysterious door.

"For God's sake, don't go too near to it!" exclaimed some of the young ladies. But the majority thought it would be great fun to see what was hidden there. Most of the men said that they considered it foolish not to have opened the door long ago and examined the room. The young bridegroom did not join in this opinion, however. He upheld the decision of his mother-in-law not to allow any attempt from anybody or persons who insist or attempt to enter into the room. He knew that there was a clause in the title deeds to the house, which made the express stipulation that no owner should ever permit the corner room to be opened. There was debate among the guests as to whether such a clause in a title deed could be binding for several hundred years, and many doubted its validity at any time. But most of them understood why Madame

Wolff did not wish any investigation, even should any of those present have sufficient courage to dare the curse and break open the door.

"Nonsense! What great courage is necessary for that?" exclaimed Lieutenant Flemming Wolff, a cousin of the bride of the evening. This man had a terrible reputation. He was known to live mostly on debt and pawn tickets, and drive pleasure in being quarrelsome. As a fighter, he was feared because of his specialty. This was the ability, and the inclination, through a trick in the use of the foils, to disfigure his opponent's face badly, without at all endangering his life. In this manner he had already sadly mutilated several brave soldiers, police officers and civilians, who had had the bad luck to stand up against him. He himself was anything but pleasant to look upon, his natural appearance having been rendered repellent by a life of low debauchery. He harbored a secret grudge against the bridegroom and bitter feelings toward the bride, because the latter had so plainly shown her dislike for him when he had tried to court her.

The family had no desire to avoid such a disagreeable relative, and had therefore sent him an invitation to the wedding. They had taken it for granted that, under the circumstances, he would prefer to stay away. But he had appeared at the ball, and, perhaps to conceal his resentment, he had been the most tireless dancer of the evening. At the meal, he had freely drunk the strongest wines, and the effect of it was plainly showing in him by this time. His eyes rolled wildly, and those who knew him took care not to oppose him, or to have anything to say to him at all.

With a boastful laugh, he repeated his assertion that it didn't take much courage to open a sealed door, especially when there might be a fortune concealed behind it. In his opinion, it was cowardly to let oneself be frightened by a centuries-old legend. He wouldn't let that bother him if he had influence enough in the family to win the daughter and induce the mother to give a ball in the haunted hall. With this last hit, he hoped to arouse the young husband's choler. But the latter merely shrugged his shoulders and turned away with a smile of contempt.

Lieutenant Wolff fired up at this, and demanded to know whether the young husband intended to call him, the lieutenant's, courage into question by his behavior.

"Not in the slightest, when it is a matter of obtaining a loan, or of mutilating an adversary with a trick during a fight," answered the bridegroom angrily, taking care, however, that neither the bride nor any of the other ladies should hear his words. Then he continued in a whisper: "But I don't believe you'd have the courage to remain here alone and in darkness, before this closed door, for a single hour. If you wish to challenge me to a fight for this doubt, I am at your disposal as soon as you have proven me wrong. But I choose the weapons."

"They must be chosen by lot, sir cousin," replied the lieutenant, his cheek pale and his jaws set. "I will expect you to have breakfast tomorrow morning at eight o'clock."

The bridegroom nodded and took the other's cold, dry hand for an instant. The men who had overheard the short conversation looked upon it as a meaningless incident, the memory of which would disappear from the lieutenant's brain with the vanishing wine fumes.

The ball was now over. The bride left the hall with her husband and several of the guests who were to accompany the young couple to their new home. The lights went out in the old house. The door of the dancing hall had been locked from the outside. Lieutenant Flemming Wolff remained alone in the room, having hidden himself in a dark corner where he had not been seen by the servants, who had extinguished the lights and locked the door. The night watchman had just called out two o'clock when the solitary guest found himself, still giddy from the heavy wine, alone in the great dark hall in front of the mysterious door.

The bride instructed the servants to make sure all the windows are completely: this was in other not to allow the Lieutenant spring out to safety in case of whatever he may encounter there or in case fear makes him change his mind and decide not to solve the mystery of the sealed room. But next morning all the windows in the great hall were found closed, just as the servants had left them the night before. The night watchman reported that he heard a hollow-sounding crash in that unoccupied part of the house during the night. But that was nothing unusual, as there was a general belief in the neighborhood that the house was haunted.

For hollow noises were often heard there, and sounds like coins falling on the floor, and rattling and clinking as of a factory machine. Enlightened people explained these sounds as echoes of the stamping and other natural noises from a small factory just behind the old house. But in spite of these explanations and their eminent feasibility, the dread of the unoccupied portion of the house was so great that not even the most reckless male servant could be persuaded to enter it alone after nightfall.

Next morning at eight o'clock Winther appeared at his mother-in- law's door, saying that he had forgotten something of importance in the great hall the night before. Madame Wolff had not yet woke up, but the maid who let in the early visitor noticed with surprise that he had a large pistol sticking out of one of his pockets.

Winther had been to his cousin's apartment and found it locked. He now entered the great hall, and at first glance, thought it empty. To his alarm and astonishment, however, he saw that the sealed door had been broken open. He approached it with anxiety, and found his wife's cousin, the doughty fighter, lying pale and lifeless on the ground. Beside him lay a large stone which had struck his head in falling and must have killed him at once. Over the door was a hole in the wall, just the size of the stone. The latter had evidently rested on the upper edge of the door, and must certainly have fallen on its opening. The unfortunate man lay half in the mysterious chamber and half in the hall, just as he must have fallen when the stone struck him.

The formal investigation of the closed room was made in the presence of the police authorities. It contained nothing but a small safe which was built into the wall. When the safe had been opened by force, an inner chamber, which had to be broken open by itself, was found to contain a number of rolls of gold pieces, many jewels and numerous notes and I. O. U.'s. The treasure was covered by an old document. From this latter, it was learned that the owner of the house some hundred years ago had been a silk weaver by the name of Flemming Ambrosius Wolff. He was said to have lent money on security for many years, but had died apparently a poor man, because he had so carefully hidden his riches that little of it was found after his death.

With a extreme stinginess that bordered on madness, he had believed that he could hide his treasure forever by shutting it up in the sealed room. The curse over the door was to frighten away any venturesome mortal, and further security was given by the clause in the title deed.

The universally disliked Lieutenant Flemming Wolff must have had many characteristics in common with this disagreeable old ancestor, to whose treasure he would have taken away secretly if he had not lost his life in the discovering of it. The old miser had not hidden his wealth for all eternity, as he had hoped, but had only delayed the inheriting of it by Madame Wolff, the owner of the house, and the next of kin. The first use to which this lady put the money was to tear down the uncanny old building and to erect in its stead a beautiful new home for her daughter and son-in-law.

The Prudent Lover

Her name is Koosje van Kampen, and she lived in Utrecht, that is most attractive of the attractive part of the cities, the Venice of the North.

All her life had been passed under the shadow of the grand old Dom Kerk; she had played little bo-peep behind the columns and arcades of the ruined, moss-grown cloisters; had slipped up and fallen down the steps leading to the canal; had once or twice, in this very early life, been fished out of those same slimy, stagnant waters had wandered under the great lindens in the Baan, and gazed curiously up at the stork's nest in the tree; had danced and laughed, had quarrelled and wept, and fought and made friends again."

But that was a long time ago, and now she had left her tomboy childhood behind her, and had become a maid-servant — a maid of refined upbringing and manners, a very dignified maid-servant indeed—with a good income annually.

She lived in the house of a professor, whose residence is at the heart of the most glamorous part of the town, one of the most influential parts of that wonderfully rich city; and once or twice every week you might have seen her, if you had been there, busily engaged in mopping the red tile and blue slate pathway in front of the professor's house. You would have seen that she is very pleasant to look at, this Koosje, very decent and clean in whatever she does and at all times. On

Sundays, she usually dresses up in her very best gown, and takes a leisurely walk along the beautiful path towards the canal, after duly going to church service every Sundays regularly. She is a member of the choir of the grand old Gothic cathedral. During the week she wore the same costume as every other servant in the country: a skirt of black stuff, short enough to show a pair of very neat-set and well-turned ankles, clad in cloth shoes and knitted stockings that showed no wrinkles; over the skirt a bodice and a kirtle of lilac, made with a neatly gathered frilling about her round brown throat; above the frilling five or six rows of unpolished garnet beads fastened by a massive clasp of gold filigree, with a spotless white cap on her head—as neat as she usually is.

It is on Sundays that Koosje always appear in an appealing gown, different color each Sunday, with her jewelleries on — a lovely ear-rings to match the clasp of her necklace, a light chain and a cross to match, one or two rings on her fingers; while on her head she wore an immense forget-me-not cap.

Then, indeed, she was a young person to be treated with admiration, and with admiration she was undoubtedly treated. As she passed along the quaint, resounding streets, many heads always turned to look at her; but Koosje walk on her way like the staid maiden she was, impressed with the fact that she is the head servant of Professor van Dijck, the most celebrated authority on the study of Osteology in Europe. So Koosje never paid any attention to the looks, or turned her head neither to the right nor to the left, but went sedately on her business or pleasure, whichever it happened to be.

It was not likely that such a treasure could remain long unnoticed and unsought after. Most people knew what a treasure Professor van Dijck had in his faithful Koosje. However, as the professor conscientiously raised her wages from time to time, Koosje never thought of leaving him.

But there is one allure no woman can resist—the allure which is love is presented romantically. As Professor van Dijck had expected and feared, that such was long held out to Koosje, and like every other young woman, Koosje is too weak to resist it. Not that he wished her to resist such. If the girl had a chance of settling well and happily for life, he would be the last to dream of throwing any obstacle in her way. He is now an old man himself; he lived all alone, except for his servants, in a great, rambling house, whose enormous apartments were all set out with horrible anatomical preparations and grisly skeletons; and, though the impressive passages were paved with white marble and led into rooms which would easily have accommodated crowds of guests, he keeps no friends except for very few of his fellow researchers in the same field; in other words, he is an old bachelor who lived entirely for research in his profession. Yet the old professor had residues of splendid memory; he recalled the time when he had been young—the time when his heart was a good deal more tender, his blood a great deal warmer, and his imagination very much more easily stirred than nowadays. There was a dead-and-gone romance which had broken his heart, sentimentally speaking—a romance long since crumbled into dust, which had made him find comfort in his study of osteology and the music of the Stradivari; yet this memory made him considerably more lenient to Koosje's weakness than Koosje herself had ever expected him to be.

Not that she had intended to tell him at first; she was only twenty-three years old, and, though Jan van Der Welda is a fine guy, and had good wages and something put by, Koosje was by no means inclined to rush headlong into matrimony. It was more pleasant to live in the professor's pleasant house, to have delightful walks arm in arm with Jan under the trees towards the canal, or parting under the stars with many lingering words and promise to meet again. It was during one of those very partings that the professor suddenly became aware, as he walked placidly home, of the change that had come into Koosje's life.

However, Koosje told him blushingly that she did not wish to leave him any time soon; so he did not trouble himself about the matter. He was a wise man, this old authority on osteology, and quoted oftentimes, "Sufficient unto the day is the evil thereof."

So the courtship sped smoothly on, seeming for once to contradict the truth of the old saying, "The course of true love never did run smooth." The course of their love so far seems to ruin Marvellously smooth indeed. Koosje, if a trifle modest, was pleasant and sweet; Jan, a fine guy as ever, always waited round a corner at cold winter night. So brightly, the happy days slipped by, when suddenly a change took place in the professor's household, which, as might be expected, also changed Koosje's life. It happened like this:

Koosje had been on an errand for the professor,—one that had kept her out of doors for some time,—and it happened that the night was bitterly cold; the weather was indeed fearful. The air had that damp rawness so noticeable in the climate of that region. A thick mist overhung the city, and a drizzling rain came down with steady persistence, the kind that can quickly soak through the stoutest and thickest clothes. The streets were almost empty due to the weather, and as Koosje hurried along into another big street—for she had a second task to perform there—she drew her clothes more tightly round her, muttering angrily, "What a weather! Yesterday was so warm, to-day so cold. 'Tis enough to give one a fever."

She delivered her message, and ran on home as fast as her feet could carry her, when, just as she turned the corner into the street that lead to her home, a fierce gust of wind, accompanied by a blinding shower of rain, assailed her; her foot caught against something soft and heavy, and she fell.

"O my God!" she ejaculated, blankly. "What fool has left a bundle out on the path on such a night? Pitch dark, with half the street lights out, and the rain and mist enough to blind one."

She gathered herself up, rubbing elbows and knees vigorously, casting a glance at the offensive bundle which had caused the disaster. Just then, lights at the streetlight came back and shed its rays through the fog upon Koosje and the bundle, from which, to the girl's horror and dismay, came a faint moan. Quickly she drew nearer, when she perceived that what she had believed to be a bundle was indeed a woman, apparently in the last stage of exhaustion.

Koosje tried to lift her; but the dead-weight was beyond her, young and strong as she was. Then the rain and the wind came on again in fiercer gusts than before; the woman's moans grew louder and louder, and Koosje did not know what to do as she had never had such an experience before.

She struggled on for the few steps that lay between her and the professor's house, and then she pressed the doorbell which resounded through the echoing passages, bringing alerted Dortje, the other maid, who ran to the door in a hurry believing that something is wrong do to the manner in which the bell was ringing. She uttered a cry of relief when she perceived it was only Koosje, who, without giving her any explanation, dashed past her and ran straight into the professor's room.

"O professor!" she gasped out; her breath was utterly gone. Due to her efforts and struggles to move the woman and her race down the passage,

The professor looked up from his book and his coffee-tray in surprise. For a moment, he thought that Koosje, his domestic treasure, had altogether taken leave of her senses; for she was streaming with water, covered with mud. Her head and cap were in a state of disorder, in such a state that neither he nor anyone else had ever seen her in since the last time she was fished out of the lake.

"What is the matter, Koosje?" he asked, studying her gravely over his spectacles.

"There's a woman outside—dying," she panted out. "I fell over her."

"You had better try to get her in then," the old gentleman said, in quite a relieved tone. "You and Dortje must bring her in. Dear, the poor soul! But it is a dreadful night."

The old gentleman shivered as he spoke and drew a little nearer to the tall white electric heater.

It was, as he had said a minute before, a terrible night. He could hear the wind beating about the house and rattling about the casements and moaning down the chimneys; and to think any poor soul should be out on such a night, dying! My God preserves others who might be belated or houseless in any part of the world in such a weather!

He fell into a fit of thoughts,—a habit not uncommon with learned men,—wondering why life should be so different with different people; why he should be in that warm, handsome room, with its soft rich hangings and carpet, with its beautiful furniture of carved wood, its pictures, and the rare decorations scattered here and there among the grim array of skeletons, which were his delight. He wondered why he should take his coffee out of costly and valuable Oriental breakable plates, sugar and cream out of antique silver, while other poor souls had no food at all, and nothing to take it out of even if they had. He wondered why he should have every luxury, and this poor creature should be dying in the street amid the wind and the rain. Life was all so unfair.

It was very unfair, the professor argued, leaning his back on his chair; it was very odd indeed. He began to feel that, grand as the study of osteology undoubtedly is, he ought not to permit it to become so engrossing as to blind him to the study of the greater philosophies of life. His reverie was, however, broken by the abrupt reentrance of Koosje, who by this time was a trifle less breathless than she had been before.

"We have got her into the kitchen, professor," she announced. "She is a child—a mere baby, and so pretty! She has opened her eyes and spoken."

"Give her some coffee or soup and some food—hot," said the professor, without stirring.

"But won't you come and check her?" she asked.

The professor hesitated; he hated attending in cases of illness because all his efforts are focused on researches, though he is a properly qualified doctor and in an emergency should lay his prejudice aside.

"Or shall I run across for Dr. Smit?" Koosje asked. "He would come in a minute, only it is such a night!"

At that moment a fiercer gust than before rattled at the casements, and the professor laid aside his principles.

He followed his housekeeper down the chilly, marble-flagged passage into the kitchen, where he never went for months together—a cosey enough, pleasant place, with a deep valance hanging from the mantel-shelf, with many great cooking pans, bright and shining as new gold, and furniture all scrubbed to the whiteness of snow.

In an arm-chair sat the rescued girl—a slight, golden-haired thing, with wistful blue eyes and a frightened air. Every moment she caught her breath in a half-hysterical sob, while violent shivers shook her from head to foot.

The professor went and looked at her over his spectacles, as if she had been some curious specimen of his favourite study; but at the same time he kept at a respectful distance from her.

"Give her some soup or coffee," he said, at length, putting his hands behind him. "Some soup and coffee—hot; and put her to bed."

"Is she then to remain for the night?" Koosje asked, a little surprised.

"Oh, don't send me away!" the golden-haired girl broke out in a voice that was positively a wail, and clasping a pair of pretty, slender hands in piteous supplication.

"Where did you come from?" the professor asked, much as if he expected she might suddenly jump up and bite him.

"From Beijerland sir," she answered, with a sob.

"Hum! Koosje, she is remarkably well dressed, is she not?" the professor said, glancing at the costly lace head-gear, the heavy gold head-piece, which lay on the table together with the great gold spiral ornaments and filigree pendants—a dazzling head of richness. He looked, too, at the girl's white hands, at the rich, crape-laden gown, at their delicate beauty, and a shower of waving golden hair, which, released from the confinement of the cap and head-piece, floated in a rich mass of glittering beauty over the pillows which his servant had placed beneath her head.

The professor was old; the professor was wholly given up to his profession, which he jokingly called his sweetheart; and, though he cut half of his acquaintances in the street through inattention and the shortness of his sight, he had eyes in his head, and on occasions could use them. He therefore repeated the question.

"Very well dressed indeed, professor," returned Koosje, promptly.

"And what are you doing in here—in such a plight as this, too?" he asked, still keeping at a safe distance.

"O my God, I am all alone in the world," she answered, her blue misty eyes filled with tears. "My dear, good, kind father died a month ago, and I am indeed desolate. I always think he was rich, and to these things," with a gesture that included her dress and the ornaments on the table, "I have ever been accustomed because he has always brought such for me when he was alive. Thus when he died, I ordered without consideration such clothes as I thought needful. And after paying for it was when I found out that there was nothing left for me—not a dime to call my own when all was paid."

"But what brought you to here?"

"He sent me here. During his illness, which lasted only three days, He instructed me gather all together and come to this city, where I was to ask for a Mrs Baake, his cousin."

"Mrs Baake, of the Cigar Factory," said Dortje, in an aside, to the others. "She employed me as one of her servant before I came here."

"I had heard very little about her. Only my father had sometimes mentioned his cousin to me; they had once been betrothed," the stranger continued. "But when I reached Utrecht, I found she was dead—two years ago; but we had never heard of it."

"Dear, dear, dear!" exclaimed the professor, pityingly. "Well, you had better let Koosje put you to bed, and we will see what can be done for you in the morning."

"Am I to make up a bed?" Koosje asked, following him along the passage.

The professor wheeled round and faced her.

"She had better sleep in the guest room," he said, thoughtfully, regardless of the cold which struck to his slippered feet from the marble floor. "That is the only room which does not contain specimens that would probably frighten the poor child. I am very much afraid, Koosje," he concluded, doubtfully, "that she is a pampered child; and what we are to do with a pampered child, I can't think of any."

With that, the professor shuffled off to his cozy room, and Koosje turned back to her kitchen.

"He'll never think of marrying her," mused Koosje, rather blankly. If she had spoken the thoughts to the professor himself, she would have received a very emphatic assurance that, much as the study of osteology had blinded him to the affairs of this workaday world, he was not yet so thoroughly foolish as to join his 'fossilised' wisdom to the ignorance of a child of sixteen or seventeen.

However, the following day, matters assumed a somewhat different aspect. Gertrude van Floote proved to be not exactly a woman of high class. It is true that her father had been a well-to-do man for his station in life, and had very much spoiled his one motherless child. Yet her education was so slight that she could do little more than read and write. The professor later found out that she had been but a distant relative of the Madam Baake, the one she had came to find, and that she had no other relative upon whom she could depend—a fact which accounted for the profusion of her jewellery, all her golden trinkets having descended to her as heirlooms.

"I can be your servant, sir," she suggested. "Indeed, I am a very useful girl, as you will find out if you will give me a chance."

Now, as a rule, the professor does not admit young servants into his house. The once he has ever tried have proved not to be cautious in their duties. They broke his breakables; they disarranged his bones; they meddled with his papers and made general havoc. So, in truth, he was not very willing to have Gertrude van Floote as a permanent member of his household, and he said so.

But Koosje had taken a liking to the girl; and having an eye to her own departure at no very distant date,—for she had been engaged more than two years now,—she pleaded so hard to keep her, promising to train her in all the professor's ways, to teach her the value of lab breakables and osteologic specimens, with a good deal of grumbling, the old gentleman gave way, and, being a wise as well as an old gentleman, went back to his studies, dismissing Koosje and the girl alike from his thoughts.

Just at first Truide, poor child, was charmed.

She put away her splendid ornaments, and normal servant uniforms were purchased for her. Her box, which she had left at the train station, supplied all that was necessary for Sunday.

It was great fun! For an entire week, the young girl danced about the rambling old house, playing at being a servant. Then she began to grow a little wary of it all. She had been accustomed, of course, to performing such domestic duties—the care of breakables, of washing and drying the clothes with the washing machine, the dusting of rooms, and the like; but she had done them as a house owner, not as a servant. And that was not the worst; it was when it came to dirty her pretty feet during work, and her having to mop the floor, clean the windows and the pathway and the front of the house, that the game of maid-servant began to assume a very different aspect. When, after having been as free as air to come and go as she chose, she was only permitted to attend service on Sundays, and to take an hour's leisurely walk with Dortje, who she consider being dull, heavy and stupid, she began to feel desperate; and the result of it all was that when Jan van der Welde came, as he was accustomed to do nearly every evening, to see Koosje, Miss Truide, from sheer longing for excitement and change, began to make eyes at him, with what effect I will endeavour to show.

At first, Koosje noticed nothing. She was so faithful naturally that an idea, a suspicion, of Jan's faithlessness never entered her mind. When the girl laughed and blushed and dimpled and smiled, when she cast her beautiful blue eyes at the big young guy, Koosje only thought how pretty she was, and even pitied her that she was not born into a family of high class.

And thus this went on for weeks. Never very demonstrative herself, Koosje saw nothing. Dortje, for her part, saw a great deal; but Dortje was a woman of few words, one who quite believed in the saying, "If speech is silver, silence is gold; " so she held her peace.

Dortje Truide, rendered fairly frustrated by her enforced confinement to the house, grew to look upon Jan as her only chance of excitement and distraction; and Jan, a thick-headed noodle of six feet high, was totally confused about what to do. A strange, mad, fierce passion for Truide had taken possession of him, and an utter distaste, almost dislike, had come in place of his old love for Koosje. Truide was unlike anything he had ever come in contact with before; she was so fairy-like, so light, so delicate, so dainty. Against Koosje's plumper, more mature charms, she appeared to the infatuated young man like—nothing he have ever seen or heard of that he compared her in his own ignorant heart to an angel. Her feet were so tiny, her hands so soft, her eyes so expressive, her waist so slim, her manner so bewitching! Somehow, Koosje was altogether different; he could not endure the touch of her heavy hand any more, the tones of her less refined voice; he grew impatient at the denser perceptions of her mind. But all this was very foolish, very short-sighted of him; for the hands of Koosje, though heavy, were clever and willing; the voice, though a trifle coarser in accent than Truide's childish tones, would never lie to him; the perceptions, though not brilliant, were the perceptions of good, every-day common sense. It really was very foolish of him, for what charmed him most in Truide was only her little polished outwards attributes (her appearance) and a certain ease of manner which doubtless she had caught from her exposure to numerous modern day entertainment which was at her beck and call when her father was alive. She had not half the excellent good qualities and steadfastness of Koosje that is needed to face everyday life; but Jan was in love, and did not stop to reason the matter seriously, as you or I am able to do. But we all know that any man in love, even the so-called wise and great men,—is often like Jan van der Welde. They lay aside for the time being the entire amount of wisdom they possess, or rather it seems that any wisdom they ever posses usually goes on tour to a remote and uninhabited island, be it great or small. And it must be remembered that Jan van der Welde was neither a wise nor a great man.

Well, in the end there came what the French call un denouement, (an ending)—what we in contemporary modern English would call a smash,—and this is how it happened. It was one evening toward summer that Koosje's eyes were suddenly opened, and she became aware of the free-and-easy familiarity of Truide's manner toward her betrothed lover, Jan. It was a very trivial thing that led her to notice it, but in an instant, the whole truth flashed across her mind.

"Leave the kitchen!" she said, in a tone of authority.

But it happened that, at the very instant she spoke, Jan was furtively holding Truide's fingers under the cover of the tablecloth; and when, on hearing the sharp words, the girl would have snatched them away, he, with true masculine instinct of opposition, held them fast.

"What do you mean by speaking to her like that?" he demanded, an angry flush overspreading his dark face.

"What is she to you?" Koosje asked indignantly.

"Maybe more than you are," he retorted;

“Wait a minute, are you two having a secrete affair right under my nose?” Koosje asked, with rage.

“Secrete? My dear Koosje, wake up, I am too old for a secret affair but to answer your question: she in my sweet darling angel,” He said with a reckless air of pride. On hearing this, Koosje was so shocked and lost for words that she marched out of the kitchen, leaving them alone.

To say she was indignant would be, but very mildly, to express her feelings; she was furious. She knew that the end of her romance had come. No thoughts of reconciling with Jan entered her mind; only a great storm filled her heart until it was ready to burst with pain and anguish.

As she went along the passage, the professor's bell sounded, and Koosje, being close to the door, went abruptly in. The professor looked up in mild astonishment, quickly enough changed to dismay as he caught sight of his valued Koosje's face, from out of which anger seemed in a moment to have thrust all the bright, comely beauty.

"How now, my good Koosje?" said the old gentleman. "Is aught amiss?"

"Yes, professor, there is," returned Koosje, all in a blaze of anger, and moving, as she spoke, the tea-tray, which she initially took up but set down upon the oaken buffet with a bang, which made its fair and delicate freight jingle again.

"But you needn't break my china, Koosje," suggested the old gentleman, mildly, rising from his chair and getting into his favourite attitude before the heater.

"You are quite right, professor, I am sorry about that" returned Koosje, curtly; she was sensible even in her trouble.

"And what is the trouble?" he asked, gently.

"It's just this, professor," cried Koosje, setting her arms akimbo and speaking in a high-pitched, shrill voice; "you and I have been warming a viper in our bosoms, and, viper-like, she has turned round and bitten me."

"Is it Truide?"

"Truide," she affirmed, disdainfully. "Yes, it is Truide, who if not for me would have been dead by now of hunger and cold—or worse. And she has been making love to that great fool, Jan van der Welde,—great oaf that he is,—after all I have done for her; after my dragging her in out of the cold and rain; after all, I have taught her. Ah, professor, but it is a vile, venomous viper that we have been warming in our bosoms!"

"I must beg, Koosje," said the old gentleman, sedately, "that you will exonerate me from any such proceeding. If you remember rightly, I was altogether against your plan to keep her in this house." He could not resist giving her that little dig, even through a kind hearted man as he was.

"Serves me right for being so soft-hearted!" thundered Koosje. "I'll be wiser next time I fall over a bundle and leave it where I find it."

"No, no, Koosje; don't say that," the old gentleman remonstrated gently. "After all, it may be a blessing in disguise. God sends all our trials for some good and wise purpose. Our heaviest afflictions are often good, most times, Koosje, because it often reveals hidden future calamity or leads to some glorious end which, while the cloud of adversity hangs over us, we are unable to discern."

"Ah!" sniffed Koosje, scornfully.

"This oaf—as I must say, you justly term him, for you are a good clever woman, Koosje, as I can testify after years of experience—but he, on the other hand, has proved to lack common sense; he has shown that he can throw away substance for shadow (to say the truth, that poor, pretty child would make a sad wife for a poor man); yet it is better you should know it now than at some future date, when—when there might be other ties to make the knowledge more bitter to you."

"Yes, that is true," said Koosje, passing the back of her hand across her trembling lips. She could not shed tears over her trouble; her eyes were dry and burning, as if anger had scorched the salty water up before they could fall. She went on to pick up the cups and saucers, and other articles the professor had used for his tea; and after a few minutes' silence, he spoke again.

"What are you going to do? Punish her, or turn her out, or what?"

"I will let him—marry her," replied Koosje, with a portentous nod.

The old gentleman couldn't help laughing. "You think that's punishment enough for both of them?"

"Before long," answered Koosje, grimly, "she will find him out—as I have done."

Then, having finished picking up the tea-things, which the professor had shuddered to behold in her angry hands, she whirled herself out of the room and left him alone.

"Oh, women—these women!" he cried, in confidence, to the pictures and skeletons. "What a mystery they are! An old bachelor is the only person to escape such, I do believe. But oh, Jan van der Welde, what a donkey you must be to get yourself mixed up in such a broil! and yet—ah!"

The fossilised old gentleman broke off with a sigh as he recalled the memory of a certain dead-and-gone romance which had happened—goodness only knows how many years before—when he, like Jan van der Welde, would have thrown the world away for a glance of a certain pair of blue eyes, at the request of a certain subtle tongue, whose broken vernacular was the sweetest music he have ever heard on earth, sweeter even than the strains of any orchestra when from under his skilful fingers rose the perfect melodies of old masters. Ay, but that sweet eye had been closed in death many long, long, year, the sweet voice hushed in silence. He had watched the dear life drift away, the fire in the blue eyes fade out. He had felt each day that the clasp of the little fingers was less close; each day he had seen the outline of the face grow sharper; and at last a time came when the poor little woman look at him with a gaze of one who does not know him anymore, and babbled, not of a baby but of the great Titanic going down in mid-Atlantic.

Ay, but that was many, many years ago. His young, blue-eyed love stood out alone in life's history, a thing apart. Of all the women, generally, the old professor had not seen any of her equal, the one woman over whose memory hung a bright halo of romance.

Fifteen years had passed away; the old professor of osteology had passed away with them; and in the large house lived a baron, with half a dozen noisy, happy, healthy children,—young bachelors and Young masters,—who scampered up and down the marble passages, and fell headlong down the steep, narrow, unlighted stairways, to the imminent danger of dislocating their fragile little necks. There was a new race of neat maids, clad in a similar neat livery uniform, who scoured and cleaned, just as Koosje and Dortje had done in the old professor's day. You might, indeed, have heard the selfsame names resounding through the echoing rooms: "Koosje! Dortje!"

But the Koosje and Dortje were not the same. What had become of Dortje, I cannot say; but on the left-hand side of the bustling, beside the picturesque worn with age canal there is a rich, beautiful shop filled with all manner of cakes, sweeties, confections, and liquors. In that shop is a beautiful, prosperous, middle-aged woman, well dressed and well mannered, no longer Professor van Dijck's Koosje, but the Madam Koosje.

Yes; Koosje had come to be a prosperous businesswoman of splendid position, respected by all. But she was Koosje van Kampen still; the romance which had come to so disastrous and abrupt end was sufficient for her life. Many proposals had been made to her, and up till now more are still proposing; but she had always declared that she have had enough of lovers—she had found out their real value.

I must tell you that at the time of Jan's infidelity, after the first flush of rage was over, Koosje refuse to show any sign of grief or regret. She was very proud, far too proud to let those close to her imagine she was miserable on account of Jan's unfaithfulness; and when Dortje, on the day of the wedding, remarked that for her part she had always considered Koosje remarkably cool on the subject of matrimony, Koosje, with a careless out-turning of her hands, palms uppermost, answered that she was right.

Very soon after their marriage, Jan and his young wife left town for another city, where Jan had promises of higher wages; and thus they passed, as Koosje thought, completely out of her life.

"I don't wish to hear anything more about them, if—you—please," she said, severely and emphatically, to Dortje.

But not so. In time, the professor died, leaving Koosje the large legacy with which she set up the handsome shop; and several years passed on.

It happened one day that Koosje was sitting in her shop sewing. In the large inner room a party of ladies and men were eating cakes and drinking chocolates and beverages with a good deal of fun and laughter, when the door opened timidly, thereby letting in a gust of bitter wind, and a woman crept fearfully in, followed by two small, crying children.

Could the lady please give her something to eat? She asked; they have had nothing during the day, and the little ones were almost famished.

Koosje, who was very charitable, lifted a tray of large, plain buns, and was about to give her some, when her eyes fell upon the poor beggar's faded face, and she exclaimed,

"Truide!"

Truide, for it was she, looked up in startled surprise.

"I did not know, or I would not have come in, Koosje," she said, humbly; "for I treated you very badly."

"Very badly," returned Koosje emphatically. "Then where is Jan?"

"Dead!" murmured Truide, sadly.

"Dead! so—ah, well! I suppose I must do something for you. Here Yanke!" opening the door and calling, "Yanke!"

"I am coming," a voice cried in reply.

The next moment, a maid came running into the shop.

"Take these people into the kitchen and give them something to eat. There is some soup and ham. Then come here and take my place for a while."

"Yes mama," said Yanke, disappearing again, followed by Truide and her children.

Then Koosje sat down again and began to think.

"I said," she mused, presently, "that night that the next time I fell over a bundle I'd leave it where I found it. Ah, well! I'm not a barbarian; I couldn't do that. I never thought, though, it would be Truide."

"waiter," was called from the inner room.

"I am coming sir," jumping up and going to her customers.

She attended to their wants, and presently led them out.

"I never thought it would be Truide," she repeated to herself, as she closed the door behind the last of the customer. "And Jan is dead—ah, well!"

Then she went into the kitchen, where the miserable children—girls, both of them, and pretty had they been clean and less forlornly clad—were sitting quietly on a chair.

"So Jan is dead," began Koosje, seating herself.

"Yes, Jan is dead," Truide answered.

"And he left you nothing?" Koosje asked.

"We had nothing for a long time," Truide replied, in her sad, crushed voice. "We didn't get on very well; he soon got tired of me."

"That was a weakness of his," remarked Koosje, drily.

"We lost five little ones, one after another," Truide continued. "And Jan was fond of them, and somehow it seemed to make him sour. As for me, I was sorry enough at the time, God knows, but what did it change? But Jan said it seemed as if a curse had fallen upon us; he began to wish you back again, and to blame me for having come between you and him. And then he took to drinking, and then to wish for something stronger; and he started smoking hemp and other kinds of weeds, and once or twice he beat me, and then he died."

"Just like that," muttered Koosje under her breath.

"It is very good of you to have fed and warmed us," Truide went on, in her faint, complaining tones. "Many people would have let me starve, and I should have deserved it. It is very good of you and we are grateful; but 'tis time for us to go, Koosje and Mina," then added, with a shake of her head, "but I don't know where."

"Oh, you'd better stay," said Koosje, hurriedly. "I live in this big house all by myself, and I dare say you'll be more useful in the shop with Yanke—if your tongue is as glib as it used to be, and I believe you still know some foreign languages, too, don't you?"

"A little," Truide answered, eagerly.

"And after all," Koosje said, philosophically, shrugging her shoulders, "you saved me from the beatings and the starvings and the rest. I owe you something for that. Why, if it hadn't been for you, I should have been silly enough to have married him?"

And then she went back to her shop, saying to herself:

"The professor said it was a blessing in disguise; God sends all our trials to work for some grand purpose. Yes; that was what he said, and he knew most things. Just think, if I were trailing about now with those two little ones, with nothing to look back to but a schnapps-drinking husband who beat me! Ah, well, well! Things are best as they are. I don't know that I ought not to be very much obliged to her—and she'll be very useful in the shop."

The End

Death Keeper

Here is a very serious reason, my dear sisters, why at last, after an absence of twenty years in a foreign country, I am confiding to you this strange secret in the life of our beloved and lamented father, and of the old house where we were children together. If I must inform you that the doctors told me that I have only a few days to live.

It is not right that this secret should die with me, my dear sisters. Though it will seem terrible to you, as it was to me, it will enable you to understand our good father better. It will also help you to understand what must have seemed strange in his inconsistencies in character. My indolence and childish curiosity was what led to my discovery of this secret.

For the first, time in my life with shame and a hotly chiding conscience I yielded to that insatiable curiosity and I peeped and listened through a keyhole, even though I did not regret it but that will be the last time I ever did such a thing because what I discovered quenched my insatiable curiosity—and when you have completely read this confession, you will understand why I do not regret that inexcusable, furtive act.

I was only a boy when we went to live in that odd little house. You remember it stood on the outskirts of the town, near the new cemetery, and was roughly boarded on the side with a deep close to the highway. You remember that on the first floor, were the room of our father, the dining room, and the children's room. In the rear of the house was the sculpture studio. There we had the large white hall with gigantic windows, where white-clothed hired works perform their duty. They mixed the plaster, made forms, chiseled, scratched. There in that large hall had our father worked for thirty years.

When I came back for the holidays, I noticed changes in our father's countenance. His beards were now white, even when he was not working with the plaster. Through his spectacles, his strong eyes glittered peculiarly. He was less calm now than he used to be. And he did not speak much, but read more than even. We all knew that after the passing away of our mother, he became a bookworm, reading very often, even in the night, using a reading light until morning.

About four days after my arrival, did this event took place. I spent my leisure hours in the studio; I carved little figures, formed little pillar heads from the white plaster. In the corner, a big plastic drum stood filled with water. It was noon; the hired workers went to lunch.

I sat down behind the drum and was carving a Corinthian pillar. Father came into the studio and did not notice me. He carried in his hands two plates of food. When he came into the studio, he closed the door behind him and looked around in the shop, as though to make sure he was alone. As I have said, he did not notice me. I was astonished at that behavior so I Held my breath and listened. Father went through the large hall, and then opened a small door, of which I knew only so much that it led into a chamber three steps lower than the studio.

I was full of expectation: I listened. I did not hear a word of conversation. Presently father came back with the empty plates in his hands. Someone bolted the chamber's door behind him.

Father went out of the studio, and I was so surprised, crept out from behind the barrel.

I knew that the chamber had a window, which looked back toward the fields. I ran out of the studio and around the house. Much to my astonishment, the chamber's window had curtains inside. A large yellow plaid curtain hid everything from view. But I had to go, anyway, for I heard Irma's voice calling from the yard:

"Antal, lunch is ready!"

I sat down at the table with you, my sisters, and looked at father. He was sitting at the head of the table, and ate without saying a word.

Day after day I was troubled about this mystery in the chamber, but said not a word to anybody. I went into the studio, as usual, but I did not notice anything peculiar. Not a sound came from the chamber, and when our father worked in the shop with his ten hired workers, he passed by the small door as if beyond it there was nothing out of the ordinary.

On the next Thursday, I should be travelling back to school. So on Tuesday night, curiosity seized me again. Suddenly I felt that perhaps never would I know what was going on in my father's house if I do not make deliberate investigation about it. That night, when the working people were gone, I went into the studio. For a long time, I was lost in my thoughts. All kinds of romantic ideas passed through my head while my gaze rested on that small mysterious chamber door.

It was already dark in the studio, and from under the small door on a thin border a yellow radiance poured out. Suddenly, I regained my courage. I went to the door and listened. Somebody was speaking. It was a man's voice, but I did not understand what he was saying. I put my ear on the door, but suddenly I heard steps at the front of the studio. Father is coming.

I quickly withdrew myself behind the barrel. Father walked through the hall and knocked on the door softly. The bolt clicked, and the door opened. Father went into the chamber and closed the door immediately and locked it.

Now all discretion and sense of honor in me came to an end. Curiosity mastered me. I knew that last year, one part of this small room had been partitioned off and was used as a woodhouse. And I knew that there was a possibility of going into the woodhouse through the yard.

I went out, therefore, but found the woodhouse was closed. Driven by trembling curiosity, I ran into the house, took the key of the woodhouse from where it is hung, and in a minute, through the split between two planks, I was looking into that mysterious little room.

There was a table in the middle of the room, and beside the wall were two mattresses. On the table a lighted candle stood. A bottle of wine was beside it, and around the table were sitting father and two strangers. Both the strangers were all in black. Something in their appearance froze me with terror.

Without knowing why, I fled in a panic and terror, but being devoured by curiosity I returned as soon as I have calmed down, to the same spot.

You, my sister Irma, must remember that unknowns to me, you followed me in there and I was startled when suddenly I found you beside me, gazing with starting eyeballs on the same mysteriously terrifying scene — and how I did not allow you to comprehend what was going on but drew you away with a laugh and a trifling explanation, so that I might return and resume my ghastly vigil alone.

One of the strangers wore a coat and had a sunburned, brown face. He was not an old man, not more than forty-five or forty-eight. He seemed to be a businessman in his ceremonial new clothes. That did not interest me much.

I looked at the other old man, and then a shiver of cold went through me. He was a famous medical doctor, a professor, Mr. H——. I want to make it clear to you that I was sure it was him and you remember that he used to come to our house for mother's treatment when she was alive, but before that day I saw his obituary on the daily newspapers two weeks ago, I even searched for it on the internet and confirms he had died and was buried! Through other news dailies on-line. And at the moment I was looking at him, sitting in the chamber of a poor plaster sculptor, in the chamber of my father behind a bolted door!

I was aware of the fact that the doctor and father are close friends. You can still recall that when father had asthma, he consulted Mr. H——. Moreover; the professor visited us very frequently. The papers said he was dead and buried, yet here he was!

With a beating heart and in terror, I looked and listened.

The professor put some shining little thing on the table.

"Here is my diamond shirt stud," he said to my father. "It is yours."

Father pushed the jewel aside, refusing the gift.

"Why not, my friend? You have been spending money on me," said the professor.

"It makes no difference," replied father; "I can't take the diamond."

Then they were silent for a long time. At length, the professor smiled and said,

"The pair of cuff buttons which I had from Prince Eugene I presented to the watchman in the cemetery. They are worth a thousand."

And he showed his cuffs, from which the buttons were missing. Then he turned to the sunburned man.

"What did you give him, General Gardener?"

The tall, muscular man unbuttoned his suit.

"Everything I had—my gold chain, my scarf pin, and my ring."

I did not understand all that. What was it? Where did they come from? A horrible presentiment arose in me. They came from the cemetery! They are wearing the very clothes in which they were buried!

What had happened to them? Were they only apparently dead? Did they awake? Did they rise from the dead? What are they looking for here?

They had a very low-voiced conversation with father. I listened in vain. Only later on, when they got warmed with their subject and spoke more audibly, did I understand them.

"There is no other way," said the professor. "Put it in your will that the coroner should pierce your heart through with a knife."

Do you remember, my sisters, that for no reason father requested for this in his last will, which was thus executed?

Father did not say a word. Then the professor went on, saying,

"That would be a splendid invention. Had I been living till now, I would have published a book about it. Nobody takes the Indian fakir seriously here in Europe. But despite this, the buried fakirs, who are two months underground and then come back into life, are very serious men. Perhaps they are more serious than ourselves, with all our scientific knowledge. There are strange, new, dreadful things for which we are not yet mature enough.

"This is the method I died; I understand it now. The mental state in which they reach systematically I reached accidentally. The solitude, the absorbedness, the lying in a bed month by month, the gazing upon a fixed point hour by hour—these are all self-evident facts with me, a deserted misanthrope.

"I died as the Indian fakirs do, and if I were not a descendant of an old wealthy family, who keep a tradition of never embalming or keeping any of our family member in a mortuary but we have a private tomb in this country were we are buried immediately after death, I would have died really.

"God knows how it happened. I don't think there is any use of worrying ourselves about it. I have only four days left. Then we go for good and for all. But no coming back, no, no, not back to life!"

He pointed with his hand toward the city. His face was burning from fever, and he knitted his brows. His countenance was horrible at this moment. Then he looked at the man with the sunburned face.

"The case of Mr. Gardener is quite different. This is an ordinary physician's error. But he has less than four days. He will be gone tomorrow or positively the day after tomorrow."

He grasped the pulse of the sunburned man.

"At this minute, his pulse beats a hundred and twelve. You have a day left, Mr. Gardener. But not back. We should never go back. Never!"

Father said nothing. He looked at the professor with seriousness, and fondly. The professor drank a glass of wine and then turned toward father.

"Go to bed. You have to get up early; you are still officially and technically alive; and you have children to live for. We shall sleep if we can do so. It is very likely that General Gardener won't see another morning. You must not witness that."

Now father began to speak, slowly, reverently.

"If you, professor, have to send word—or perhaps Mr. Gardener — somebody we must take care of, a command, if you have—"

The professor looked at him sternly, saying but one word:

"Nothing."

Father was still waiting.

"Absolutely nothing," repeated the professor. "I have died, but I still have four days. I live those four days here, my dear old friend, with you. But I won't be going back any more. I don't even need to turn my face backward. I don't care to know how others I have left behind live. I don't want life, old man. It is not honorable to go back. Go, my friend—go to bed."

Father shook hands with them and disappeared. General Gardener sat stiffly in his chair. The professor gazed into the air.

I began to comprehend all that had happened here. These two apparently dead men had come back from the cemetery, but how, in what manner, by what means? I don't understand it perfectly even now. There, in the small room, facing towards the cemetery, they were living their few remaining days. They did not want to go back again into life.

I shuddered. During these few minutes, I seemed to have learned the meaning of life and of death. Now I myself felt that the life of the city was at a vast distance. I had a feeling that the professor might be right. It was not worthwhile. I, too, felt tired, tired of life, like the professor, the feverish, clever, serious old man who came from the coffin and was sitting there in his grave clothes waiting for the final death.

They did not speak a word to each other. They were simply waiting. I did not have the power to move away from the crack in the wall through which I saw them.

What followed after this was the awful thing that drove me away from our home, never to return.

It was about half-past one when someone tapped on the window. The professor was alarmed and looked at Mr. Gardener with a warning to take no notice. But the tapping grew louder. The professor got up and went to the window. He lifted the yellow curtain and looked out into the night. Quickly he returned and spoke to General Gardener, and then both went to the window and spoke with the person who had knocked. After a long conversation, they lifted the man through the window.

After this terrible day, nothing could happen again that would ever surprise me. I was benumbed. The man who was lifted through the window was clad in white linen to his feet. He was a religious man, a poor, thin, weak, pale man. The man wore a white funeral dress. He shivered from the cold, trembled, and seemed almost unconscious. The professor gave him some wine. The man stammered,

"Terrible! Oh, horrible!"

I learned from his broken language that he had not been buried yet. He had not yet known the smell of the earth. He had come from his bier.

"I was laid out a corpse," he whimpered. "My God, they would have buried me by tomorrow!"

The professor gave him wine again.

"I saw a light here," he went on. "I beg you, will you give me some clothes—something to eat, if you please—and I am going back home again." Then he said in a foreign language,

"Meine gute, theure Frau! Meine Kinder!" (My good wife, my children.)

He began to weep. The professor's countenance changed to a devilish expression when he heard this lament. He despised the lamenting man.

"You want to go back?" he thundered. "But you won't go back! Don't shame yourself!"

The man gazed at him stupidly.

"I live in Rottenbiller Street," he stammered. "My name is Joseph

Braun."

He bit his nails in his nervous agitation. Tears filled his eyes.

"Ich muss zu meine Kinder," he said in foreign language again, which I interpret to be German. (I must go to my children.)

"No!" exclaimed the professor. "You'll never go back!"

"But why?"

"I will not permit it!"

The man looked around. He felt that something was wrong here. His startled manner seemed to ask: "Am I in a lunatic asylum?" He dropped his head and said to the professor simply,

"I am tired."

The professor pointed to the mattress.

"Go to sleep. We will speak further in the morning."

Fever blazed in the professor's face. On the other mattress.

General Gardener now slept with his face to the wall.

The man staggered to the mattress, threw himself down, and wept. He was shook terribly by the weeping. The professor sat at the table and smiled.

Finally, the man fell asleep. Hours passed in silence. I stood motionless, looking at the professor, who gazed into the candlelight. There was not much left of it. Presently he sighed and blew it out. For a little while there was dark, and then I saw the dawn penetrating the yellow curtain at the window. The professor leaned back in his chair, stretched out his feet, and closed his eyes.

All at once, the man got up silently and went to the window. He believed the professor was asleep. He opened the window carefully and tried to creep out. The professor leaped from his chair, shouting,

"No!"

He caught the man by his shroud and held him back. There was a long knife in his hand. Without another word, the professor pierced the man through the heart.

He put the limp body on the mattress, then went out of the chamber toward the studio. In a few minutes, he came back with father. Father was pale and did not speak. They covered the dead man with a rug, and then, one after the other, crept out through the window, lifted the corpse out, and carried it away. In a quarter of an hour, they came back. They exchanged a few words, from which I learned that they had succeeded in putting the dead man back on his bier without having been observed.

They shut the window. The professor drank a glass of wine and again stretched out his legs on the chair.

"It is impossible to go back," he said. "It is not allowed."

Father went away. I did not see him anymore. I staggered up to my room, went to bed, and slept immediately. The next day, I got up at ten o'clock. I left the city at noon.

Since that time, my dear sisters, you have not seen me. I don't know anything more. At this minute, I keep saying to myself that what I saw that day, which is what I have set down here, doesn't sound like the truth. Maybe it never happened; maybe I have dreamed it all. My mind is not clear. I have a fever.

But I am not afraid of death. Here, on my hospital bed, I see the professor's feverish but calm and wise face. When he grasped the man by the throat he looked like a lover of Death, like one who has a secret relation with the passing of life, who advocates the claims of Death, and who punishes who ever want to cheat Death.

Now Death urges his claim upon me. I have no desire to cheat him—

I am so tired, so very tired.

God be with you, my dear sisters.

The End

Generational Curse

There were many wonderful things that aroused our childish fantasy when Balint Orzo and I were boys, but none aroused our curiosity so much as the old tower that stands a few feet from the castle, shadowy and mysterious. It is an old, strange, square tower, and at the brink of its notched edge there is a shingled helmet which was erected by one of the late Orzos.

There were so many legends told about this old tower. A rumor exists that it has a secret chamber into which none is permitted to enter, except the head of the family. Some great secret is concealed in the tower-room, and when the first-born son of the Orzo family becomes of age, his father takes him there and reveals it. And the effect of the revelation is such that every young man who enters that room comes out with gray hair.

As to what the actual secret might be, there was much conjecturing. One legend had it that once some Orzo imprisoned his enemies in the tower and starved them until the prisoners ate each other in their crazed suffering.

According to another story, Kelemen Orzo ordered his faithless wife Krisztina Olaszi to be plastered alive into the wall of the room. Every night since then, sobbing is heard from the tower.

Another runs that every hundred years a child with a dog's face is born in the Orzo family and that this little monster has to live all its live in the tower and even perish in the tower-room, so as to hide the disgrace of the family.

Another theory was that once the notorious Menyhart Orzo, played a game of checkers with his neighbor, Boldizsar Zomolnoky. They commenced to play on a Monday and continued the game and played all week until Sunday morning dawned on them. Then the family priest of the Cathedral came and pleaded with the gamblers. He begged them to stop the game on the holy day of Sunday, when all true Christians are in church praising the Lord. But Menyhart, bringing his fist down on the table in such rage that all the wine glasses and bottles danced, cried: "And if we have to sit here till the world comes to an end, we won't stop till we have finished this game!"

Scarcely had he uttered his vow when, somewhere from the earth, or from the wall, a thundering voice was heard promising to take him at his word—that they would continue playing till the end of the world. And ever since, the checkers are heard rattling, and the two damned souls are still playing the game in the tower-room.

When we were boys, the secret did not give us any rest, and we were always discussing and plotting as to how we could discover it. We made at least a hundred various plans, but all failed. It was really impossible to get into the tower, because of a heavy iron door and a chained steel burglary proof. The windows were too high to be reached. We had to satisfy ourselves by throwing a well-aimed stone, which hit the room through the window. Such an achievement was somewhat of a success, for oftentimes we drove out an alarmed flock of birds.

One day, I decided that the best way would be to find out the secret of the tower from Balint's father himself. "He is the head of the family," I thought, "and if any light is to be had on the mystery, it is through him." But Balint didn't like the idea of approaching the old man; he knew his father's temper.

However, once he did questioned his father about it but he regretted doing so afterwards, for his father flew into a rage, and scolded and yelled at him, ending by telling him that he must not listen to such nursery-tales; that the tower was moldering and decaying with age; that the floor timbers and staircase were so infirm that it would fall to pieces should anyone approach it; and that this was why no one was allowed into it.

For a long time afterwards, neither of us spoke of it.

But curiosity was incessantly working within us, and one evening Balint solemnly vowed to me that as soon as he became of age and had looked into the room, he would call for me, even if I am at the end of the world, and would let me into the secret. In order to make it more solemn, we called this a "blood-contract."

With this vow, we parted. My parents sent me to college; Balint had a private tutor and was kept at home in the castle. After that we only met on vacation time.

Eight years passed before I saw the Orzo home again. At Balint's urgent, sudden invitation, I had hurriedly journeyed back to my rocky fatherland.

I had scarcely stepped on the wide stone stairway leading from the terrace in the front of the castle, when someone shouted that the master of the house was near! He came driving at a high speed with a convertible. I looked at him and started, as if I had seen a ghost, for this thin, tall guy was the perfect resemblance to his father. The same knotty hair and bearded head, the same densely furrowed face, the same deep, calm, gray eyes. And his hair and beard were almost as white as his father's!

He came speeding through the gates, smashed the brake pedal with a sudden jerk, and the next moment was on the paving; then with one bound he reached the terrace and had me in his muscular arms. With wild eagerness, he showed me into the house and at the same time kept talking and questioning me without ceasing. Then he thrust me into my room and declared that he gave me fifteen minutes—no more—to dress.

The time had not even expired. When he came, like a whirlwind, embraced me again and carried me into the dining-room. There chandeliers and lamps were already lit; the table was elaborately decorated, and bore plenty of wine.

At the meal, he spoke again. Nervously jerking out his words, he was continually questioning me on one subject and then another, without waiting for the answer. He laughed often and harshly. After the meal, when we started to drink, he winked to the servants, and immediately five orchestra musicians entered the room.

Balint noticed the astonishment on my face, and half evasively said,

"I have sent to Vienna for them in honor of you. Let the music sound, and the wine flow; who knows when we will see each other again?"

He put his face into his palm. The orchestras played Antonio Vivaldi- Four seasons. Balint glanced at me now and then, and filled the glasses; we clinked them together, but he always seemed to be worried.

It was dawning. The soft chirp of birds from some distance rose to us.

Balint put his hand on my shoulder and bent to my ear.

"Do you know how my father died?" he asked in a husky voice. "He killed himself."

I looked at him with amazement; I wanted to speak, but he shook his head and grasped my hand.

"Do you remember my father?" he asked me. Of course; while I looked at him, it seemed as if his father were standing before me. The very fibrous, skinny figure, the muscles and flesh seeming peeled off. Even through his coat arm, I felt the naked, unveiled nerves.

"I always admired and honored my father, but we were never true intimates; I knew that he loved me, but I felt as if it was not for my own sake; as if he loved something in my soul that was strange to me. I never saw him smile; sometimes he was so harsh that I was afraid of him; at another time, he was unmanageable.

"I did not understand him, but the older I became the better did I feel that there was a sad secret germinating in the bottom of his soul, where it grew like a climbing grass, the tentacles of which crept up to the castle and covered the walls, little by little overshadowed the sunlight, absorbed the air, and darkened everyone's heart. I gritted my teeth in vain; I could not work; I could not start to accomplish anything. I struggled with hundreds and hundreds of determinations; to-day I prepared for this or that; tomorrow for something else; ambition pressed me within; I could never complete whatever I started. Behind every resolution I made, I noticed my father's countenance, like a note of interrogation. The old fables that we heard together in our childhood were suddenly renewed in my memory. Little by little, the thought grew within me, like a fixed delusion, that my father's fatal secret was locked up in that tower room. After that, I lived by the calendar and dwelt on the passing of time on the clock. And when the sun that shone on me when I was born arose the twenty-fourth time, I pressed my hand on my heart and entered my father's room—this very room.

"'Father,' I said, 'I have become of age today, everything may be opened before me, and I have the right to know everything.' Father looked at me and pondered over this.

"'Oh, yes!' he whispered, 'this is the day.'

"'I should know everything now,' I continued; ' I am not afraid of any secrets. In the name of our family tradition, I beg you, please open the tower-room.'

"Father raised his hand, as if he wanted to make me become silent.

His face was as white as a ghost.

"'Very well,' he murmured, 'I will open the tower-room for you.'

"And then he pulled off his jacket, tore his shirt on his breast, and pointed to his heart.

"'Here is the tower-room, my boy!' did he whisper in a husky voice. 'Here is the tower-room, and within our family secret. Do you see it?'

"That is all he said, but when I looked at him, I immediately perceived the secret; everything was clear before me and I had a presentiment that something was nearing its end, something about to break.

"Father walked up and down; and then he stopped and pointed to this picture; to this very picture.

"'Did you ever thoroughly look at your ancestors? They are all from the Orzos. If you scrutinize their faces, you will recognize in them your father, yourself, and your grandfather; and if you ever read their documents, which were left to us—there they are in the box—then you will know that they are just the same material as we are. Their way of thinking was the same as ours and so were their desires, their wills, their lives, and deaths. We had among them soldiers, clergymen, scientists, but not all of them were great, celebrated man, although their talent, their strength almost tore them asunder.

"'In every one of them, the family curse took root: not one of them could be a great man, neither my father nor yours.'

"Then I felt as if something horrible was coming from his lips. My breath almost ceased. Father did not finish what he was going to say, but stopped and listened for a minute.

"'I was my father's only hope,' he went on after a while; 'I too was born talented and prepared for great things, but the Orzos' destiny overtook me, and you see now what became of me. I looked into the tower-room. You know what it contains? You know what the name of our secret is? He who saw this secret lost faith in himself. For him, it would have been better not to have come into this world at all. But I loved to live and did not want to abandon all my hopes. I married your mother; she consoled me until you were born, and then I regained my delight in life. I knew what I had to keep before my eyes to bring up my son to be such a man as his father could not be.

"'I accepted reluctantly without protest, when you left for the foreign countries; then your calls came. I made a special study of every sentence and of every word you spoke, for I did not want to trust my reason. I thought the first time that the fault was in me; that I saw unnecessary phantoms. But it wasn't so, for what perceived out of your words was our destiny, the curse of the Orzos; from the way of your thinking, I found out that everything is in vain; you too turned your head backward, you too looked into yourself and noticed there the thing that makes the perceiver sterile forever. You did not even notice what you have done; you could not grasp it for your reason, but the poison is already within you.'

"'It cannot be, father!' I broke out, terrified.

"But he sadly shook his head. 'I am old; I cannot believe in anything now. I wish you were right, and would never come to know what I know. God bless you, my son; it is getting late, and I am getting tired.'

"It struck me that he was trying to cover his disbelief with sarcasm. Both of us were without sleep that night. At dawn, there was silence in his room. I bitterly thought, 'When will I go to rest?' When I went into his room in the morning, he was lying in his bed. All was over. He had taken poison and written his farewell on a piece of paper. His last wish was that no one should ever know under what circumstances he died."

Balint left off speaking and gazed with outstretched eyes toward the window in the darkness. I slowly went to him and put my hand on his shoulder. He started at my touch.

"I more than once thought of the woman who could be the mother of my son. How many times have I been tempted to fulfill my father's last wish? But at such a time, it has always come to my mind that I too might have such a son, who would cast into his father's teeth that he was a coward and a selfish man; that he sacrificed a life for his illusive hopes.

"No! I won't do it. I won't do it. I am the last of the Orzos. With me, this damned family will die out. My fathers were cowards and rascals. I do not want anybody to curse my memory."

I kissed Balint's wet forehead; I knew that this was the last time I would see him. The next day I left the castle, and the day after, his death was made public. He committed suicide, like his father. He was the last Orzo, and I turned about the coat of arms above his head.

The End,

About the Author

Henry Carter is an author of fiction for adults. He also writes tales for children. He is currently focused in 'excavating, refurbishing and rebranding' lost or forgotten short stories from authors around the world, these include short stories series which goes with the title: The immature Lover, The accidental wife, I am too good for my husband, The billionaire proposal and The battle for inheritance, with still more to come on the series.

He also writes non-fiction books on subjects ranging from Common sense to compilations of Wits and Jokes.

Henry is one of those mature bachelor living very close to you, who cooks his own meals. He is still trying to get married but keeps deceiving himself that there is still time. Anyway, if you ask for a plate of his dishes, he is not stingy about that.

You can reach him through his email:
Okeyjedi@gmail.com

The Authors

The Immature Lover Original Story by **Lucy Maud Montgomery** Titled: **The Martyrdom of Estella**

The Amateur Lover original Story by **Guy de Maupassant** Titled: **The Son**

Neglected Necessity original Story by **Erckmann - Chatrian** Titled: **A Forest Betrothal**

The Adoption Original Story by **Guy de Maupassant** Titled: **Adoption**

The Gold Digger- Original Story By **Fiodor M. Dostoyevsky** Titled: **The Christmas Tree and the Wedding**

The Stolen skeleton Arm Original Story by **Jorgen Wilhelm Bergsoe** Titled: **The Amputated Arms**

Enigmatical Manuscript Original Story by **Otto Larssen** Titled: **The Manuscript**

The Mysterious Room Original Story By **Bernhard Severin Ingemann** Titled: **The Sealed Room**

The Prudent Lover Original Story by **John Strange Winter** Titled: **KOOSJE: A Study of Dutch Life,**

Death Keeper Original Story by **Ferencz Molnar** Title: **The Living Death** from Hungarian Mystery Stories

Generational Curse original Story By **Arthur Elck** Titled: **The Tower Room**

www.ingramcontent.com/pod-product-compliance
Lightning Source LLC
La Vergne TN
LVHW091312150826
845673LV00006B/1615